THE MARROW
OF THE WORLD

RUTH NICHOLS
...

THE MARROW
OF THE WORLD

Illustrated by Trina Schart Hyman

A MARGARET K. MCELDERRY BOOK

Atheneum 1972 New York

To Richard Fariña
The running sands recall the time

THE MARROW
OF THE WORLD

1

"No, Linda!" Philip spoke forcefully, curbing his impatience. "I'm responsible for your safety, and you're not used to the scuba gear. I won't let you go down."

She turned on him, her jade eyes gray with anger. Even in the ordinary print blouse and cotton shorts she looked oddly wild, her brown face thin and vivid. She was two years younger than he: Philip loved her, quarrelled with her and called her his cousin, though he knew his aunt and uncle had adopted her from an orphans' home when she was very small. All this summer she had been spiteful and termagant.

"I'm going to dive!" Linda's hand, fine-boned as a bird's claw but unexpectedly strong, gripped the wooden side. The rowboat rocked beneath them.

"You're hateful sometimes, Linda. What's been wrong with you this year?"

He crushed his fingers around her wrist, and she sat still. Her face held some quality of waiting: anger sheathed and poised. Philip spoke quickly. "It may be dangerous! Whatever it is, it wasn't there last year."

"But how can that be?" she whispered. "The walls are ruined: they must be hundreds of years old!"

They were silent. Around them the rich stillness of August lay over the lake where they spent their holidays. Beneath the boat, green-brown water; on every side the rock shores crusted with lichen, gray as hardened smoke, and mantled with pines. Here and there a maple stood rooted, its leaves flaring orange or autumn-rose against the green. In two weeks it would be time to go home.

Linda turned her head. From here she could see the roof of her parents' cottage: there were no others on the lake. Her black hair had dragged free from its ribbon and fell like tangled silk over her arms. She heard the oars creak in their metal sockets.

"Let's move a little further." Philip rowed a few

4

feet through the water and they drifted into stillness again. He whistled softly. "Rooms and rooms!
What a labyrinth."

"How deep is the water here?"

"Forty feet."

"You'll go down, then."

"Yes."

Without Philip's needing to say it, she knew he
was afraid. Waves slapped and sucked against the
sides of the boat. Near the surface the water was
pale, translucent brown, deepening to amber,
through which the black shapes of minnows
darted. And only a few feet down, the walls began.

They were crumbled walls, their thickness mellowed to gold by the rippling water-light. Rowing
slowly, Philip and Linda had traced the outlines of
corridors, of one great chamber, and a honeycomb
of smaller rooms. The walls sank down and down
into blue-green shadow.

"They seem so near the surface I could reach
down and touch them," murmured Linda.

"You couldn't: it's deeper than you think."
Philip shook his head. "We swam here last summer. There was nothing on the bottom then."

She watched in silence as he pulled on the flip-
pers and adjusted the diving mask. He stepped out
of the boat and sank, feet first, into the water; and
Linda was alone.

For a long time she waited. Wind stirred the

hair around her head; her hands lay loosely in her lap. At the far end of the lake another boat was moving, as Linda's father rowed back and forth; she could see the sunlit curve of a fishing-rod.

Then Philip's head broke the surface, and his fingers gripped the boat's side. "Get over there to balance it while I climb back in."

A moment later, sitting on the board seat, he pulled off the mask, tossed it down and shook the water from his hair. For an instant he stared at Linda. Then he said: "There's nothing there."

"What?" The word was a whisper.

"I said there's nothing there. There are no walls. The bottom's smooth: not even any weeds."

The silence lengthened into minutes. "But I can *see* them!" said Linda at last.

Her cousin shrugged. "So can I."

Around them the water glittered, rippling and pleating like silk. And below, wavering but distinct, lay the walls.

Linda drew a breath. "All my life," she said softly, "I've wanted something magical to happen."

She turned to him. "We'll come back tonight, after dark, and bring the electric torch. I want to see if they'll still be here."

"After dark! You're crazy, Linda: I won't let you!"

"How will you stop me, then?"

"If need be, I'll tell your parents."

Suddenly she smiled, and the smile was almost gentle, almost gay. "You know you won't do that."

Philip made no answer. He would not, of course. He would not tell on Linda or betray this secret, however she might anger him.

From their earliest childhood, his devotion to Linda had amused and bewildered the adults around them. "What draws them together?" he had once overheard his Aunt Margaret say, "They're so different!" Philip knew that in a curious way he envied Linda her arrogance, her quick temper, her assurance. These qualities, so foreign to his own cautious, thoughtful nature, sometimes angered, sometimes fascinated him: always they brought him back to be her champion.

And there was another reason, which as yet he scarcely understood. Beneath the character she wore for Philip and for everyone else, there lay a loneliness that Linda never spoke of. But now and then Philip glimpsed it in her face, and it filled him with uneasy pity.

The house where they spent their summers was made in the form of one great room, which rose like a varnished shell over the braid rugs and white wicker chairs of the living-area, and over the low partition walls. Anything said in one room could be heard in most of the others. One of the

7

few places a private conversation was possible was the screened-in porch where the family ate their meals. Here, at dusk, Philip went to look for his aunt.

As he came through the screen-door and down the step, his uncle was just turning away. "We'll have fish for breakfast, then, Margaret."

"Did you catch anything?" asked Philip.

"Three lake trout." His uncle grinned, and measured their length with his hands. "Right over the place where you two were rowing about. It's a pity you didn't take the chance to do some fishing. Well, I'll be back by dark."

In silence Philip absorbed the knowledge that his uncle had crossed that same area of the lake, and had seen nothing.

When he had gone, Philip came and sat down beside his aunt, who was sewing at the table. She glanced up at him and smiled. "Philip, will you light the Coleman lantern?"

He lit it and hung it from the hook in the ceiling, where the brilliant, hissing light fell full on her work. Outside he could see the blue of dusk and hear the murmuring voice of the lake.

Linda was sitting alone on the dock. Philip and his aunt could see the hair that fell over her shoulders like a silken veil. Suddenly she straightened, her whole body filled with a sharp, unchildish grace. Philip felt a constriction of alarm.

"Aunt Margaret, where does Linda come from?"

"From the asylum, Philip: you know we adopted her." His aunt was gentle and blue-eyed, with blonde hair falling in curls and wisps about her cheeks. She gave a faint, anxious frown. "I know I needn't ask you not to talk to her about it. We wouldn't want to say anything that might make her feel . . ."

Philip nodded. "Of course. I mean *before* the asylum. Did they ever tell you that?"

"You know institutions don't release that kind of information."

"But you did make inquiries once, didn't you?"

There was an instant's pause; then his aunt nodded. "Yes. After she started talking about the wolf."

Philip remembered. The dream Linda had told him about again and again: the dream in which she found herself alone, walking out into a plain of rustling, sun-bleached grass. It was dark, and mountains lay far on the horizon. Then out of the far distance came a wolf, running soundlessly. It circled her, its eyes two pools of iridescent gold; then it vanished toward the mountain-range from which it had come.

"And what did you find out?" he said after a moment.

She shook her head. "Nothing."

"They wouldn't tell you?"

"They didn't know."

She laid down her sewing and looked at him. "Philip, they didn't *know* where she came from. She was found, abandoned. They tried to trace her parents, and when no one could be located they put her up for adoption. Unless they lied to us, that's all they know."

Philip leaned down and gently kissed her cheek. "She does love you, Aunt Margaret."

Her smile was troubled. "Does she?"

Supper was over. The dishes had been cleared away, and the Coleman lantern shone over the table. Its light was now the only illumination, except for a candle that Linda had set upright in a saucer.

They were taken up with the evening's quiet occupations: Philip and his aunt reading, his uncle working on his fishing lures, surrounded by penknives and glue and balls of twine. Linda, her forehead wrinkled in a frown of boredom, was drawing with crayons on a sheet of blue paper. Philip drew a deep breath of contentment, savoring the smells he associated with this house: the odors of timber, of oilcloth and kerosene.

A shadow fluttered between him and the light. A moth had somehow found its way into the room; now it was swooping raggedly, circling ever nearer to the flame. Philip saw that his cousin too was watching it, her gray eyes as clear, as mysterious as water.

"Linda, snuff the candle," he said. "The silly thing's going to burn itself!"

She moved to obey, but it was too late. Blinded, the insect flew into the candle flame and died. Linda gave a whimper of horror, and, to Philip's astonishment, burst into tears.

"Linda, what is it?" exclaimed her mother.

"The moth! The moth!"

"Well, dear, next time you'll know not to set a candle on the table."

"I've seen it somewhere," whispered Linda.

"Seen what?"

Philip saw his aunt grow tense, saw her husband look up cautiously. They had heard such things before.

"Seen it where, Linda?"

She shook her head, her face twisted into a grimace of anger. "I don't know! There was a woman, who—who let insects die like that. Only it wasn't moths, it was fireflies. She imprisoned them in a green glass lamp, and their light was beautiful."

"Where did you see this, Linda?" her mother persisted gently.

But Linda had regained self-control. Her grief had slipped back into the secrecy where she was content to hide it, as she hid many other thoughts and feelings, Philip suspected. "Perhaps I dreamt it."

"You have too many dreams."

Linda made no answer, but cast her mother a look of contempt. Pushing back her chair, she got up from the table. They heard her footsteps cross the darkened living room; then her bedroom door closed, and the latch clicked into place.

There was silence for a moment among the three left behind. Philip saw that his aunt was quietly weeping. With a swift, impatient gesture, she brushed the tears away, then spoke to her husband as though Philip were not there. "Jim, what are we going to do?"

It had been dark now, Philip guessed, for almost five hours. It would not be so very long before a faint, cold dawn began to stain the horizon above the trees. Already several times his awareness had been cancelled by moments of dark and silence, and he knew he had been asleep.

He lay fully clothed on his bed in the little cubicle, divided only by a partition from Linda's parents' room. He could hear the night-sounds: the scuffling of a squirrel's feet among the drifted pine needles on the roof; the occasional sharp crack as a chair or wooden beam settled in the cold. He was weary and angry at the thought that Linda had forgotten, that she had not meant what she said about going out again on the lake at night, or that she had been teasing him.

At that instant his door opened and Linda stood beside him. She gripped his shoulder and gently shook it; she did not need to warn him to silence. In the darkness he could see the dull gleam of metal: the powerful electric torch she had taken from the cupboard where her father kept his fishing-tackle. Philip frowned at a brief, unpleasant memory.

They had been only children that year, and Hallowe'en was approaching. Linda's parents had forbidden her to buy firecrackers: her father said they were dangerous. Aunt Margaret had sent them both to the store on some errand; and as Philip searched for the articles on her list, he had seen Linda gazing with longing intensity at the packages of firecrackers, wrapped in their red and orange tissue and tied with strips of printed paper. As he looked, she reached forward and stealthily slid one of the packages into her coat pocket.

She saw him watching her. She winked and turned away to look at the licorice and peppermints in their glass jars on the counter.

Afterwards he had called her a thief. But she only laughed, and he had never told her parents; for he loved Linda too much to betray her, and so he let her go her own way, even when it distressed him and she appeared not to care.

13

Now she was barefoot and wore a sweater. Once again Philip noticed the extraordinary silence with which she could move when she wished. She led him across the living room and down into the porch. From across the partition came a stirring, a sleepy murmur, and then silence. Philip and Linda eased the screen door shut behind them. Only when they were outside did they stop to put on their shoes.

In the time before dawn the night was at its deepest and most silent. In two more days the moon would have waned toward its brief vanishing. Now it was no more than a silver-brown shadow in the sky. The stars outshone it, still furnaces of light, each burning with a cold brilliance. In spite of his thick pullover, Philip felt his body contract into a shudder, partly with cold, partly with awe at the night around them. The sky was black, as a country sky can be when it is not blurred by the light-haze of a city. Even the branches and the waves were still.

He followed Linda down the short slope to the boathouse. Now they were inside, among the echoes, the odors of rotting wood and acrid, sun-scorched rubber. Starlight glittered in the mesh of a spider's web woven across the door-lintel. Linda switched on the torch. Its beam pierced downwards, shafting a core of golden water, stirred by yellow weed and the darting bodies of fish. By its light they climbed down into the rowboat.

Cautiously they rowed out into the darkness: Philip at the oars, Linda sitting in the bow with the torch to guide him. Mostly they rowed in darkness, for fear that the light might be seen by someone wakeful in the house. Philip found himself caught between pleasure and anger. He did not attempt to deny that he was beginning to enjoy the adventure, the blackness and the velvet silence. But it angered him that he should have let Linda have her way, willful and unreasonable as it was. He seldom let her bully him, though she tried.

Because the house was unlit, its roof soon vanished into shadow, and it was as if they found themselves alone on a lake in the wilderness. "Do you think there are bears?" whispered Linda, glancing at the black shore and jagged trees.

"Perhaps," said Philip. If it frightened her, he thought fiercely, so much the better.

They were now in the middle of the great shadowed lake. "Right about here, I think," murmured Linda, and switched on the torch. It caught only an instant of black water.

Philip shook his head. "Over toward the shore a bit."

They were now cruising, as near as they could judge, directly over the place where they had seen the walls. At the thought of what might lie beneath them Philip felt himself begin to shake again, this time with fear. He could tell nothing of what Linda was feeling from her still intensity.

Once or twice she switched on the light and searched the water with it. Philip could see nothing in its beam but waves rippling, slick as satin. Linda stirred fretfully. "I can't see anything." She still spoke little above a whisper, though there was no one else to hear. "The light doesn't pierce the water: it's as if it won't let light through. That's strange."

She extinguished the light again and they sat for a moment in silence, their broad, shallow boat riding on the waves. "Listen!" said Philip suddenly. "What's that?"

He could feel the sudden tension of her alertness in the darkness opposite. A second later the sound came again: a plop, a swirl of water, and a gleam of phosphorescence. "Only a fish," whispered Linda.

Her cousin shook his head. "Whatever it is, it doesn't need our light: it's making its own."

They waited.

Suddenly the boat rocked. Philip grasped the sides; and at the same instant a figure of ghostly brightness came shimmering up from the depths of the lake and broke the surface not four feet from the rowboat. Linda's cry was stifled in her throat, for the face that gazed at them was human: its hair sleek as an otter's, its dark eyes sheathed

with lids of an oriental fold. Between its long fingers, smoothly stirring the water, beat webs of transparent skin.

Then it sank from sight. Again the rowboat swayed, and both Philip and Linda hung on to maintain their balance. It was as if, thought Philip, the water had been stirred by the motion of a powerful tail—a tail as thick as a man's legs.

For an instant they were silent, trembling. "Let's get out of here!" said Philip.

He knew the merman could stop them if he chose. But he rowed strongly, and they moved with surprising speed out from the shore and back toward the headland where the cabin stood.

"Do you think it will come into deep water?" Linda's voice had lost its arrogance and was that of a frightened child.

"I can't tell," Philip replied.

Something strange was alive in the lake, and anything might happen to them before they reached the safety of the boathouse. But they rowed and saw nothing more.

Now out of the darkness Philip could distinguish the table-rock where he and Linda sometimes came to swim. They were approaching the headland. Here was the steep shore, and there the trees that hid the cabin roof. Strange: in the darkness he could see no sign of the house. But they had only to round this neck of land . . .

"What's happening?" exclaimed Linda. All at once Philip lost control of the oars. The boat was turning and veering in a swirl of water. "What's happening?" she cried again.

"A current: I don't know where it's coming from. There *is* no current here!" Philip was struggling to draw the boat into calmer water. "We should be in sight of the boathouse. What's going on?"

"You've led us wrong: we're not where we thought we were. Look, there's a stream running out of the woods, and we were heading into its mouth!"

It was true. Philip could hear the clamor of water over stones. Where the boathouse should have been, a water-channel now flowed into the lake. And it was deep and strong enough that it had driven their boat backwards.

The current was slackening now; he had regained control. A moment later they were rowing outwards again into the open water.

"Then where is the house?" he said aloud. "I was *certain*—"

"So was I. Oh, Philip, let's go ashore. Let's wait till morning. If we row around—"

He knew: moving blindly about the lake, they might have a second encounter.

"All right, we'll go ashore. We'll be in trouble when they find we've been out all night. But I'm lost." His voice fell to a whisper. "And no stream runs into this lake: not that I've ever heard of."

They drew the rowboat up onto a gravel beach, and knotted the bow-rope around the stem of a sumac bush. "Bring the boat-cushions," said Philip. "My knapsack is still under the seat, left over from the picnic yesterday. The space-blanket is in it, and some matches. Here, I'll get it."

Ten feet above the shingle, they found a shoulder of rock, crusted with brittle lichen and tangled with juniper bushes. But it was approximately level, and in the small clear space, while Linda held the torch, Philip gathered brushwood and built a fire. "We must keep it burning," he said. Linda nodded. They both knew there were bears in these forests in summer.

In the knapsack they found a sandwich wrapped in paper, one orange and a box of raisins. The sandwich was spoiled, but they broke the orange in half and shared the raisins. The sweet, shriveled fruit did not really satisfy their hunger, but left them feeling a little comforted.

Linda wore only shorts and a sweater, and she was shivering. "I'm cold."

"The space-blanket will keep us fairly warm." It was a square of plastic bonded to a sheet of metal foil, and weighed only a few ounces. It was Philip's most prized possession, next to the hunting knife whose handle had been carved from a reindeer-antler. That too he wore at his belt, since he seldom went without it. "If we turn the silver side inwards, it will conserve our body-heat. Come on, we'll use the boat-cushions as pillows."

So, on that hard and comfortless bed, they settled down side by side, close together for warmth. The sky was still black above them. They lay open-eyed, waiting and watching.

2

Still morning did not come. Philip found that all need for sleep had left him. Linda lay beside him quietly, but from time to time the starlight caught the gleam of her eyes, half-open beneath their long lashes, and he knew she was not asleep. His mind was troubled by the things they had heard and seen: the merman's shoulders and face, glimmering silver, reared above the water; the stream where no stream should have flowed into the lake.

So quietly they lay, so filled with the calm of waiting, that they made no stir or murmur when another shadow moved along the shore—a humped shape, that made the stones of the beach crunch softly beneath its weight. Philip guessed at first that it was a moose, for the great body measured eight feet at the shoulder. It paused directly below the rock-slope where they lay and bent to drink. Then Philip saw its horns.

They rose, shining bone-pale in the starlight, and curved like a giant lyre. The creature bore their weight: the movement of its haunches and shoulders, the slow turn of its head, all expressed the pride of this kingly burden. No creature Philip had ever seen wore such a crown. It bent to drink for a moment from the dark, star-sparked water; then it was gone into silence as it had come.

What can such a beast be doing here? thought Philip. *Where did it come from?* If such an animal roamed these woods, his uncle would surely have spoken of it.

To his surprise Linda said nothing. Then her arm shot up from the blanket, pointing. "Look!"

"What?" he demanded.

The stillness magnified her whisper. "Don't you see that the stars have changed?"

Philip reared back, searching the sky. The stars still shone cold and white above him, and gradually a pattern blended into awareness in his mind. From horizon to horizon a great constellation filled the sky, looped and jagged like a rope of diamonds. All around it the darkness was powdered with lesser stars, faint and glittering as mica-dust, whose light seemed worlds and centuries remote from the place where he and Linda lay. And low over the trees shone a great green star, translucent as a jewel. Of Jupiter, whose cold brilliance he was used to seeing in the autumn sky, he could find no trace.

"Something has happened, Philip." In Linda's whisper he heard a tension of delight, of exultation. "There *is* no lake, no cabin. When we wake in the morning we'll find it entirely different."

The certainty in her words made him shudder, half with anger. Throwing off the blanket, he sat up. "When we wake in the morning, we'll find ourselves in bed. This is a dream, and a bloody nightmare at that."

She gave a shrill, stifled giggle. "There! Is *that* a dream?"

Philip swore: she had leaned forward and pinched his arm. In instant retaliation, he cuffed her hard across the cheek. Linda was silent, staring at him from the black shadows of her hair.

"I'm sorry," said Philip roughly. He knew he had not struck her because of the pinch, but because her confidence and her strange delight had frightened him.

"I'm sorry too." All at once the wildness left her. "I can't help it sometimes, Philip," she said softly.

"It's all right, I tell you!" They were quiet.

Dawn came, leaching the sky to sapphire and then to apple-green. Above the far trees a bank of cloud remained. Before the cousins' eyes its color changed to primrose, then to apricot, and at last to the magnificent rose-gilt so brilliant, so instinct with light, that it could not endure beyond the brief moment of the sun's rising. Philip chafed his arms beneath the sweater; the air was sharp with chill.

"It seems a lot more like autumn than it did last night," he remarked.

Linda nodded. "You see, there's no house."

Philip turned and looked toward the headland where her parents' cabin should have stood. It was bare in the strengthening light. He knew that if he were to take the boat and row across, he would find only blueberry-scrub and juniper. The house and its inhabitants had vanished.

Loneliness filled him suddenly. His body was taut with fear and hunger, for neither he nor Linda had eaten a meal since supper the day before. As the first light struck the hills' crests, he saw trees farther gone in autumn than they had been when dusk settled down. Their leaves flamed rose and orange, with here and there a deep purple veined with red that he had never seen before.

They were in a different world. Somehow, between their rowing out from the deserted boat-house and the moment they dragged their boat up on the shingle, the transition had been accomplished. How and for what purpose he could not tell.

A sudden suspicion made him lift his head. "Linda, do *you* know why this has happened?"

He saw her begin to shake her head; but the motion froze. She was staring at something beyond him, across the narrow neck of water that divided their beach from the opposite shore. In her face Philip saw astonishment, recognition, joy, blending and changing so swiftly that he watched her in fascination. Only when several minutes had passed did he turn to follow her gaze.

From the bushes fifty feet away across the water, a great gray wolf was watching them.

There under the trees dark still lingered; a mist was coiling and steaming on the surface of the lake. Against the tree-shadows and the shadow of its body, the creature's eyes glowed amber, veined with gold.

A low cry broke from Linda: half-animal, a wordless sound of recognition. Philip knew, for she had told him, that she had seen this creature in dreams fifty times before.

At that moment the wolf turned from them and bounded away into the underbrush. "That way is west," said Linda. "He wants us to follow him."

"Follow him where?" Philip spoke as calmly as

she had done. He would need all his wits to challenge her conviction.

Linda shook her head. "I don't know."

"And what do you intend to do? Follow him in
the rowboat?"

"There's the river. I'm sure we're meant to go
that way."

"We do not know where the river leads." If they
took that road, thought Philip to himself, they
would indeed be lost in this strange world. At least
the place where they now were bore the contours
of their own familiar lake, though all landmarks
had vanished. But who could tell where the river
flowed?

"Anyway," he said firmly, "we'll make no decisions until we've had something to eat. I'm fam-
ished."

Linda nodded. Her face was very white, and her
arms, what he could see of them, were mottled
with gooseflesh in the morning chill. "So am I."

But where were they to find food? Now Philip
bitterly regretted that, while carelessly leaving his
knapsack in the boat, he had remembered to take
his fishing tackle back to the house. No berries
grew this near the lake as he knew it, and he could
see none now that the lake had changed.

"I've heard of gathering roots and herbs," said
Linda doubtfully. "And we might find some blue-
berries."

Preoccupied with their bewilderment and their hunger, neither Philip nor Linda saw a small boat gliding silently over the water, now silken with sunrise, and through the vanishing mist. When Philip looked up and gave a soft exclamation of surprise, the boatman had already seen them and, driving his paddle into the water, had brought his craft to a halt. There he sat not five yards distant, watching them.

In his own world Philip would have called the boat a canoe. Bow and stern tapered upwards, belling in the middle into a space wide enough to hold a pack and two more men. It appeared to be made of bark lashed with thongs; only this boat was made not of birch but of what looked like cinnamon-bark.

The boatman himself was no less strange as he sat regarding them shrewdly, his paddle at ease across his knees. He was small, muscular, and very dark, with black eyes and tightly curling black hair. Down to the knees he was clothed in a doeskin jacket, belted with twisted thongs and crusted with beads as fine as grains of sand. These had been worked into a pattern of flowers and tendrils and glittered faintly in the morning light; Philip saw that they were made of crystal, coral, and amber. At his belt he wore a knife, and over his shoulders a cloak of some dark fur. A necklace of bear-claws hung about his neck. All his clothes were dirty with travel and long wear.

Across the water his voice came to them, distinct but not loud. "I am Herne," he said, "that some men call the Hunter. Do you welcome chance-meeting, and do you go armed in the wilderness?"

"We have no weapons." It was Linda who answered. "We cannot defend ourselves against such a one as yourself. But we have nothing worth the plundering."

Philip glanced at her in surprise, as a suspicion he could not yet put a name to grew more insistent in his mind. She had fallen naturally into the idiom of the land: she had answered Herne in his own speech. And neither of them had spoken in English.

Herne laughed. "I am no robber. I ask merely if I may come ashore. It is strange to see a boy and a maiden alone in the forest, especially if they bear no weapons."

"Why?" said Linda. "Is it dangerous to be alone here?"

Herne nodded. "Most dangerous."

Using his paddle, he poled the canoe into shallow water and drew it up onto the beach. Philip saw that he wore mocassins and black cloth breeches. Herne sprang lightly out and stood, hands on hips, considering them. On Linda his gaze lingered an instant longer, with a trace, Philip

thought, of surprise and speculation.

"How did you come here?"

In the instant in which his mind still hovered between his own language and the unfamiliar one that came unbidden to his tongue, Philip heard the words and knew how they would have been spoken in English. He was certain now that Linda had not even noticed the transition. Then: "Forgive us," he said, "but we cannot tell you while we are faint with hunger."

For a second his memory strained to recapture the English syllables; then he was speaking and thinking in a language he had never heard before.

"That can soon be mended. Good! Your fire still burns. Pile some kindling on it." Herne turned to his pack and, unstrapping it, brought out a pan and, wrapped in leaves, a rabbit, freshly skinned. Moving swiftly, he began to cut the meat into collops against a log of wood. "Cut small, this will cook quickly. In my pouch I have some herbs to flavor it."

Half an hour later the three sat around the fire, dipping with their fingers into the savory mixture of stewed meat and herbs. It was now full daylight; all around them the lake lay peaceful in its autumn brilliance, as though no cabin had once stood there, as though no merman stirred the depths beneath the waves. Herne glanced at the rowboat. "Where do you come from? I cannot believe you have traveled far in that."

Philip and Linda exchanged a glance. They had no means of knowing what they should tell and what they should conceal. Herne cocked his brows. "You are silent."

"We are silent," said Philip at last, "because we do not know where we are or how we came here. We come from a place that has vanished."

Gradually, with many hesitations, they told him what they knew. Herne watched them intently but without astonishment. When they had finished, Linda filling in what Philip had omitted, he gave a short, positive nod. "Some power is at work: you have been brought here. That is plain enough. Such things do not occur by chance."

"But why?" demanded Philip. The word "power" filled him with a vague, sudden fear.

Herne shook his head. "I do not know. But when I saw you my first thought was that Linda, at least, was native to these woods. I have seen forest-people very like to her: my sister is one. When my eyes fell on you, I imagined for an instant that I beheld her, as she was when we were children together."

"And the wolf?" said Linda.

"I think that you should follow it. It may be you will see it again, for you say it is a creature of night, and it seems your dreams have shown you this. In such things you must trust your own under-standing."

Linda nodded.

"But that means we're letting this Power guide us!" protested Philip. "It has brought us here, and now it's leading us where it wishes us to go. Why should we follow so obediently when it may be leading us into danger?"

"Because," said Herne, "you have no choice."

Philip fell silent. It was true. To sit here on the banks of the lake would be no use, for he felt a reluctant certainty that another sunrise would not bring a return to his own familiar, reassuring world. He must go forward; to turn back was impossible.

Herne saw acquiescence in his face. "Leave your boat here; on this river it will not carry you far. I can take you in my carac for as far as our ways lie together. I am curious and will travel as close to this Power as I can."

"Mightn't that be dangerous for you?" said Linda. "Perhaps it doesn't want you."

"That may be. But perhaps my presence will shield you from danger; few know these woods as I do. And in the deep forest dwells an enemy I will take revenge on, when I can."

"Why? For what?" asked Philip.

Herne shook his head. "Perhaps some day I will tell you. But look, the sun is fully risen. We must go."

So with Linda sitting cross-legged in the belly of the carac and Philip, with the second paddle, in the bow, they pushed off from the gravel beach and headed against the current into the river's mouth. Here the boathouse should have stood. There was no sign of it, not even crumbling foundations tangled with grass and reeds. As Philip turned for a last glimpse of the lake, so strange yet so familiar, he felt a pulse of loss, of excitement, and of fear.

3

All that day and all the next, they labored up the river. Philip was used to handling a canoe, but never before for hours on end; after the first day, the pain of the muscles in his arms and shoulders was hard for him to bear. However, sometimes Linda insisted on taking his place, partly because she guessed his exhaustion, and partly because she did not like to be left out of anything. Philip was grateful to her and tried not to be jealous that she paddled tirelessly and well.

They were passing through country wilder than anything Philip or Linda had ever seen. Before many miles the deep brown channel widened, and

became a jade-green river flowing between banks of smooth white stones. Pines, dark green in day-light and blue where the shadows touched them, rose like spears into a sky hard and bright as pol-ished turquoise. They saw no living thing except an occasional hawk, riding the wind on its spread wings. The trees shut out all vision to right and left, and after a while they were aware only of blue sky, green water, and white stones.

The days still held a fragile, autumn warmth, but the nights came cold. When the first day's dusk fell, they camped on a gravel bank, and Herne, seeing that Linda was shivering with the chill, wrapped his cloak around her shoulders. Linda thanked him for it, trying not to grimace at the raw smell of the hide. The fur was indigo, so deep and brilliant she could hardly believe it had not been dyed.

"Where did it come from?" she asked, spread-ing her fingers in the soft, coarse fur.

"It is the pelt of a blue bear." Herne grinned, and touched the necklace at his throat. "These are his claws."

They had built a fire in a hollow among the rocks, and they lay quietly around it. Above them the sapphire of dusk still lingered.

"Herne," said Linda, "will you not tell us about your enemy in the forest?"

He made no answer for so long that Linda

thought he was rebuking her by silence. At last he stirred and spoke softly into the shadows of the fire. "I am not certain who my enemy is. But something in the forest captured my father and held him prisoner till he died."

The stillness was broken by Philip's soft breath of astonishment.

"Our king now," continued Herne, "is Kyril Tessarion, a great king and wizard. He fought hard to win this land from the evil things that held it. For many years before my birth, he was waging war against them, until at last these great matters touched even my father, a simple huntsman of the wilderness. For as Kyril cleared the open lands of witches and sorcerers, the few that survived his vengeance fled northwest into the forest where my father trapped and hunted and lived with his children in a house built of cedar logs.

"There was one above all: a witch named Morgan—a woman curst and beautiful. She had been a great countess, until news came to Kyril of her cruelty and sorcery and the torture of her subjects. He drove her out by power stronger than her own and freed the prisoners in her stronghold; but when his soldiers sought her, she had vanished.

"Not for many years did he hear of her again, until rumor came that a palace was rising in the wilderness, built, it was said, by the claws of beasts and birds. When it was completed, Morgan appeared once more and dwelt there openly in defiance of the King, for she felt that, so many leagues from his capital, she was safe from him. There she lived in lonely magnificence with enchanted animals as her servants. And it was said among the woodsmen that sometimes, to amuse herself, she would wander abroad in the form of a young maiden, enticing men into her stronghold to keep them prisoner. But these were only her pleasures: all her skill was bent on regaining her lost power.

"There were five of us children at that time: my three brothers, my sister, and myself (for my mother had died at the time of my sister's birth). I was the eldest, and so it fell to me to learn my father's skill in woodcraft and to watch over the younger ones.

"One day at dusk I went with my father into the margin of the forest to gather firewood for the winter. The first frost had already fallen, and on the ground the dead oak leaves crackled with a film of ice.

"My father was working some way ahead. All at once the blows of his axe fell silent, and looking up, I saw that he was staring at a woman. She was dressed in brown, a robe too light against the cold, and yet the cold seemed not to touch her. Black hair fell about her face and curtained her body to the feet. Her face was narrow, set with eyes of gray or hazel: some dark and changing color. Her skin glowed with a white light.

"I saw her lean her slender body against the stem of a winter tree, saw her smile and beckon. My father watched her as one enchanted. Then she moved away, drifting like a shadow among the trees; and he followed her. I tried to cry out, to move, but some power held me both still and silent."

For a long moment he said nothing, gazing into the fire. Then he lifted his head. "This story has no ending, for I never saw him again. Darkness fell and the power released me. I searched for my father all that night, but found no trace of him nor of the maiden. In time my brothers grew to be men, brave and skilled in woodcraft, and my sister into a fair woman. But our father never came home again.

"What later happened to the witch, I do not know for sure. Rumor came to us that only a few years since—about the time of your own birth, Linda—Kyril pursued her even into her forest castle, which stood on the shores of Lake Evaine. It was told that, rather than surrender her fortress, she blasted its walls and sank them beneath the waves. But whether the King destroyed her or whether she still lives, I cannot tell. The name of that forest is no longer so evil as once it was.

"The destruction of Morgan's castle touched my

kindred only in one way, if indeed any link exists between the King's justice and a vision my sister saw in the same year. She was alone in her husband's house, which stands in a small town on the first slopes of the downs, and it was evening. All at once she looked up from her work to see my father watching her. She says he was dressed in cloth of silver, and a blood-red jewel hung from a chain about his neck. He was tall and comely as she had known him, but in his face she saw the suffering of long imprisonment. He smiled at her and lifted his hands in the sign of blessing. The next instant there was nothing but the rosy light of evening falling through the window.

"When my sister told me this, I knew my father had been freed from the bondage in which he had been held. I also knew that he was dead."

Philip checked the words of pity that came to him: somehow silence seemed better. Tears were flowing down Linda's face. Herne reached out and gently brushed one from her cheek. "Sad chances happen to many in the world. And he was freed at last."

She nodded. After a moment she said: "I think I know now what the walls were that we saw. But I don't yet know why."

At that instant all three became aware of two lights glowing like pale flames among the trees. They looked up and saw that the wolf had returned to watch them.

A soft exclamation broke from Herne's lips. "You are guided indeed! But I wish I knew whether you are guided to good or ill."

By day they did not often see the wolf. Once or twice they glimpsed a shadow slipping among the trees, now ahead of them, now some way behind; but every night when they made camp, the eyes would watch them from the darkness the creature seemed able to create around itself. They did not approach it. All three felt certain that the beast would vanish if they came too near. Herne said: "If you approached him, you might find only a hare bounding away into the underbrush or a bird that flew up into the trees. For it may be that this is a shape-shifter, no true wolf at all."

"Can a shape-shifter assume human form?" asked Philip.

Herne shrugged. "Sometimes, depending on the power of its master. Or so it is said. My father met a shape-shifter once in the form of a black bear and slew it with fire; but for myself I have encountered only the common creatures of the wild. And," he added softly, "I was content that it should be so!"

But as long as the creature visited their camp at night, they assumed they were following the right path.

As the days went on, Philip grew hardened to the work of paddling. His body felt lighter and stronger than it had in the other world. But as they journeyed closer to the green shadow of the deepest forest and the blue shadow of the mountains, he could see that Herne was troubled. And his trouble increased Philip's own anxiety of mind. For the moment two questions could not be answered: why they had been brought here, and how it would be possible to get back. His mind exhausted itself by circling uselessly around these two questions.

And there was a deeper source of disquiet. Linda was changing. Philip could express it no more clearly than that, for the transformation as yet consisted only in a glance, in the timbre of her laugh, in the occasional gesture, when she would change in an instant from her usual quiet movements to a grace that was queenly, arrogant, and wild. Then it would vanish almost before Philip could be certain he had seen it.

She was at home in this world. Philip had guessed already that she was native to it, as Herne had surmised. The change that had translated them from their known world to this one could, Philip supposed, have worked the other way when Linda was a baby; though how, and for what reason, remained mysterious. It surprised Philip that he could make this guess so calmly. Perhaps his mind

43

had been prepared for the full strangeness of her origin by the knowledge, which he had always possessed, that she was alien to his family. Now his anxiety for her was greater than his curiosity about her birth.

On the fifth day the river ended and lost itself in a desolate marshland of stagnant water, willows, and brown reeds. Here and there a late water lily, bright as a buttercup, bloomed among the rushes, crowning a long stem gray with slime. "We must take care," Herne warned. "The water here is shallow and choked with rotting logs. Do not step out of the carac: the mud is very deep. But if we can win through, there is a water-channel some way to the north and east."

Their paddles served as poles to push the boat inch by inch, searching always for logs or mudbanks beneath the honey-colored water. All around them brown velvet bulrushes were moldering into down. Though it was late afternoon and the sky was clear, the light seemed lustreless. They could hear no sound but the wind in the reeds.

It seemed that the marshland had gradually engulfed what had once been a living forest; for now from the water reared the trunks of drowned trees. Their wood was silver-gray with disease and age. Twisted roots splayed their arms above the water, and the way was choked with fallen branches.

Linda had read about the Dead Sea where, when

the water is still, one can glimpse in its depths the cedar trunks of an ancient forest. But now the ghostly wood was all around them. She shivered. "What a horrible place!"

They were drawing near another clump of willows, which stood on a hummock of firm land. At that instant a scream tore the silence. Philip had barely time to realize that it was the voice of a bird, when a great hawk plunged down through the air and came to rest for a moment on the prow of the carac. Its lifted wings were as wide as Philip's outstretched arms; its eyes gleamed fierce as rubies.

"Down, Linda!" shouted Herne, and swept at the creature with his paddle. But he was too slow. The hawk snatched up the bow-rope in its claws and carried it, trailing and uncoiling, up into the willow branches. Herne cursed and grasped at the other end, which was knotted securely to an iron ring in the bow. Then the hawk released the rope and dropped it, snarled and tangled, among the branches. He circled above them once and, with a last cold, mocking scream, flew away over the trees.

"This is willful mischief." Herne's face was grave.

Philip drew out his knife. "We'll have to cut it down: there's nothing else to be done."

Herne shook his head "No. I can't afford to lose the rope. Do not stir. I suspect some harm. It seems a trick to make us leave the boat, perhaps so the hawk's master can steal it and abandon us here. I'll climb up and salvage as much rope as I can."

They poled the carac up close to the clump of trees. Here the water was clearer and flowed in a narrow channel. Philip glanced along it and saw that the channel extended, deep and distinct, threading its way among all the obstacles for as far as his eyes could follow it.

The boat rocked as Herne sprang from it into the bole of one of the willows, which rose in four great arms. Quickly he began to climb, his knife in his hand.

He was halfway up when all three of them heard a rushing, bubbling sound, like the noise of a swift stream. The water in the channel had foamed into sudden motion, as though it were a river distinct from the marshland all around it and under separate command. Philip looked down to see the water swirling around the carac's sides.

"Herne!" cried Linda. The current was carrying them forward, straining against the rope. From above them, they heard Herne's answering shout of anger and alarm. "The tree, Philip! Catch at the branches if you can!"

It was no use. At that instant the bow-rope snapped of its own accord, and the carac, with Philip and Linda helplessly crying out, was borne off down the deep, swiftly-moving channel.

4

"Herne!"

Linda's scream was lost in the sounds of rising wind and rushing water. Already the willows were far distant against the sky. She turned to Philip. "We could jump."

He shook his head. "The current would still carry us where it wants us to go—if it didn't drown us first."

"But Herne! What will happen to him? Will he be safe?"

"I hope so. Let's hope the Power lays no traps for him, now that it has succeeded in capturing us. Even if it does, he has a chance; he is crafty and knows the wisdom of trusting nothing in this land."

"Will we ever see him again, I wonder?" murmured Linda. Philip was silent.

Still the boat carried them on, rocking violently at times, as if jostled by invisible hands. They had left the marsh, and the forest was closing around them again. From the high, pearly light, they knew that afternoon was waning.

The sun sank, a globe of gold, into the cloud beyond the trees. Twilight fell on the river. Philip and Linda sat quietly, husbanding their strength for whatever they must meet at the end of this journey. They did not speak of it, but it comforted them to be together. Cheered by Linda's presence, Philip felt a stirring of courage, even of curiosity, to see what the end would be.

As night fell, they could discern that the river had become as it was before, but now it was narrower and the trees taller, stronger, and more ancient. No more than a yard's distance divided them from the shore on either side; but the current that bore them had great power, and they sensed that the channel, narrow as it was, was still very deep. Now, here and there, the first diamonds of the great constellation came winking out of the blue.

They did not know how many hours this lasted. At times they even slept—a light sleep, tense but refreshing—and woke to find themselves sitting upright in the boat, gazing ahead.

It was full dark when at last the current beneath them began to slacken, and the carac, turning, grated gently aground on a beach of white stones. As far as they could tell, it had brought them ashore in the deepest part of the wilderness. The forest rose before them like a wall.

"Our guide is waiting for us," Linda whispered, and slid her hand into Philip's. Her fingers were cold; he clasped them reassuringly.

"Then we've come to the right place," he said. But alone in the forest, fear threatened to overmaster his courage and even his anger at the way they had been brought here.

Before them, like darkness made visible, the wolf had materialized. Now Philip read a beckoning in its eyes, mute and cruel though they were. It led them silently, turning now and again to look back at them. Philip and Linda followed, hand in hand.

As his sight grew accustomed to the blackness, Philip realized that it was not total. He could make out the shapes of the trees. They were giants, reaching up into darkness, their girth the growth of many centuries. Here in the deepest wilderness they had grown, while in the world outside men died and kingdoms faded with the years.

There was no underbrush; their feet crunched softly over dry needles. The ghostly brightness of fireflies faded in and out of the gloom ahead, a dancing brilliance that cast brief shadows on the trunks and on the ground. Philip looked up. Far above he could see the deep, clean blue of the night sky; but here under the branches all was secret and profoundly still.

Their guide halted some way ahead. He was standing, the cousins saw, before the greatest tree of all. It rose into the night like the pillar of a giants' hall.

Then all at once the eyes went out.

"Come on," whispered Linda, and tugged at his hand.

"I'm afraid."

"Come on!"

They moved a few steps nearer to the tree. At that instant another figure took shape in the shadows and stood before them. For a second Philip thought that his heart had ceased to beat. The figure was that of a man.

And yet not a man. They knew at once that this was the shape-shifter. His clothes were black, his face shrouded. His voice was like the murmuring of the wind. "Go in. My mistress waits for you."

Then they saw that a door was set into the tree. Philip laid his hand upon the handle; he opened it and stepped through.

They were standing inside the great tree, and light shone through the web of a scarlet curtain. Linda reached out and drew the curtain aside. Again they moved forward and down a step carved in the living wood.

There came a stirring from the bed that stood by the farther wall. A woman reared up against the pillows. Her whisper was clearly audible in the silence. "So you have come!"

Philip cast one swift glance around him. The whole tree had been hollowed out to make an ample room. Far up in the dimness he could see a vaulted roof, and from it by a long chain, hung a globe of glass. This was filled with the flickering, green-white glow of innumerable fireflies. By their light he saw that the floor was made of polished wood, ringed with the circles of the tree's long growing; but the curving walls were armored with great sheets of copper, fixed to the wood by lines of silver nails. In this strange mirror his and Linda's reflections glimmered, shadows of rose and amber.

There came another stir and rustling from the bed: the woman had pushed back the quilt, which was of brown cloth embroidered with black roses, and set her feet to the ground. Her gown, like the bed curtains, was made of some thin gray stuff that glinted with fallow silver when she moved.

She was beautiful and, Philip thought for an instant, young. But her movements were feeble and her face haggard. Her hair, fine as brown silk, cascaded to the ground about her feet; but there was something in its color that reminded him of fading. She watched them, her face wavering between astonishment and triumph. Her bearing spoke of mortal sickness; yet Philip did not pity her. From that first moment he felt only dislike and fear.

She turned her beautiful, crazed eyes on Linda. Philip tensed protectively. "What do they call you?"

"Linda, madam," she answered steadily.

For a moment the woman considered this in silence. Then in uncertainty and distaste, her gaze transferred itself to Philip. "And this other?"

"My cousin Philip."

"There should not have been two of you. But I am weak, and the spell was almost beyond my strength. At first it conjured only visions of forgotten things." Now she was moving about the room, her skeletal fingers twisting and writhing together.

"You brought us here, then," said Philip.

"I did."

He gathered all his courage to express the certainty that had been growing in his mind. "And we know who you are. You are Morgan the Enchantress."

"Morgan the Enchantress!" She threw back her

head, her lips parted over small, sharp teeth. Her laugh was as harsh as the scream of a rock-falcon.

Then just as suddenly she was still. "No. Kyril destroyed my mother by fire, this day twelve years ago. He made a living torch of her, for he knew that only so can witches be destroyed. May he be curst to death and darkness for it! I am a shadow only of my mother's power and beauty. I am Ygerna." She looked again at Linda, and her voice took on a silken gentleness. "Do you not remember me, Sister?"

In all the room there was no sound but Linda's sharp, intaken breath.

"Sister?" she whispered at last.

Ygerna nodded. "You were a fortnight old when our mother received news of Kyril's approaching army. To save you, she rocked you into an enchanted sleep; and you woke in a world beyond Kyril's reach, for he would have killed you."

Linda shuddered. "Killed a child? Would he do that?"

"Most certainly. Witches and witch-children— he spares none." She halted in her pacing and gazed at Linda with a veiled expression: almost, thought Philip, a look of mistrust. "And yet you are but half a witch, a bastard. In me the strain runs true, for *my* father was of demon-blood and long lived with our mother as her husband. But your father was mortal: a poor woodsman, whom Morgan enticed for her amusement."

"It's not true!" Linda's whisper was haunted, desperate. "It's not true!"

"What says your cousin to that?" demanded Ygerna. Her eyes were turned on Philip with a look of ironic understanding. "Has she not changed since you came here?"

He felt his skin flush hot with horror and with anger. "She is not yours, Ygerna; you cannot have her! I will protect her if I can."

Her laughter mocked him. "If you can! Linda, I have brought you here to perform a service for me."

"What is that?" For the moment Linda had withdrawn into a cold calm. Yet even in her stillness Philip could see that she was searching for a means of escape.

Ygerna sank back onto the bed, back into the veil and cloak of her long hair. The weariness, which anger and triumph had quickened for a moment into life, had now returned. "We are not immortal, though legends make us so. Over the long years we grow old, and like men, we should die if we had not found a means of prolonging our lives. I myself am spent: too near death to journey to the shores of Lake Evaine, where our mother's portion of the Marrow was lost when she sank her palace beneath the waves. You will make the journey for me."

"The Marrow?" demanded Philip.

Ygerna nodded. Her words came in a hissing whisper. "The Marrow of the World!"

For a long moment she was silent. Then she moved her head against the pillow. "It is years beyond counting since all the lands were changed, since the most ancient sea was lost and sank beneath the mountains. Now its bed lies deep in the caverns of the dwarfs. Only they know the way, and they will sell the Marrow only for a great price."

"But what is it?" persisted Linda.

"The earth from which all life sprang. In its fecundity the first seeds came into being, the seeds that led to growing things, to trees, to beasts, and men. Even the oceans and the long, slow growth of stone take their birth and their first impulse from that primeval earth, now buried beyond knowledge and memory. We only remember it, and the dwarfs alone know where it may be found."

"But our mother had some?" said Linda. Philip heard with a pang of alarm the implicit admission her words contained.

Ygerna nodded. "Enclosed in a golden box, in her private chamber. I will tell you presently."

"Why should I do this for you?" Linda's voice was still and cold. "It seems to me it would be better to let you die. I have no wish to serve you. You are as evil as Morgan was."

"Can you not read your heritage, even in those words? A true witch will let her kindred die if they cannot be of use to her." All her intensity was bent on Linda; Philip stood uncomfortably by, forgotten. "And yet I can be of use to you, Linda. I alone know how to restore you to the world you have grown accustomed to if you choose to return there. And there is another reason."

"What, then?" said Philip. He could no longer conceal his anger and his hatred of her.

Ygerna spoke so softly that they strained to hear. "You are a witch. Whether you believe this truth or not, whether in this world or another, you are Morgan's daughter. Like me you will at last grow faint and sick, like me you will die. And witches, Linda, have no souls. When we die, we perish utterly."

A silence followed on her words. At last Ygerna spoke again. "Stay here and live. When I am well, I will challenge even Kyril's mastery. Stay with me and be powerful. Your other choice is to die and be extinguished, as though you had never been.

"And now," she said, "you will sleep, for I see that you are weary. In the morning I shall send you on your way. Linda will remain here with me, Philip. I have prepared another room for you."

"No!" Philip put his arm around Linda's shoulders. She was trembling pitiably, but she said nothing. "I will not be separated from Linda before we leave here."

For a moment thwarted anger distorted Ygerna's face. "I should have guessed, my sister, that in a strange world you would fall in with bad companions. Well, that cannot now be mended—though you may find you wish to rid yourself of him before the end. Come with me."

She led them toward a hole in the metal casing of the wall. Down a flight of steps they went, with curved walls above them and around them. Philip realized that the passageway had been hollowed from one of the tree's great roots: it smelled of earth and living wood.

It ended in an earthen chamber deep below the ground. The air was both cold and close, and the walls gleamed with seeping water. A mattress and quilts were spread upon the floor. "I will wake you in the morning," said Ygerna. "Sleep, if you can."

But, though beside him Linda sank at once into an exhausted sleep, Philip lay wakeful in the stifling darkness, not daring to close his eyes.

He must have slept at last, for he woke abruptly as a green shadow came wavering down the passageway. Ygerna appeared at the door. In her palm she held a lamp—a globe of emerald glass that shed a cold green light. "It is day outside. Rouse up. My servants have laid out clothes for you while you slept; you will need them for the journey. Put them on." She placed the globe-light on the floor and left them alone.

Beside him, Linda was stirring and murmuring into wakefulness. Then Philip saw that clothes had indeed been laid beside them: for Linda, a long gray gown; for himself, cloth breeches and a plain doeskin tunic like the one Herne had worn; for both, hooded cloaks of coarse brown cloth. He cursed himself for the weariness that had allowed Ygerna's servants, whatever manner of creature they might be, to approach unheard and unseen.

They dressed. Both kept their own canvas running-shoes, and Philip retained his hunting-knife with its sheath. The space-blanket, which he had treasured carefully since the day they first met Herne, he folded small and tucked in between his tunic and his belt. Then Linda knelt and carefully picked up the green glass globe. "It's cold," she exclaimed, "even though it burns!"

In the main chamber with its copper walls, the door stood open on a forest wreathed with morning mist. The fireflies lay dead on the floor of the pendant lamp. Ygerna saw Philip glance at them and smiled faintly. "They last only a night. They kill themselves by fluttering against the glass."

On a table stood white bread and apples in a wooden bowl. "Break your fast while I show you the supplies I have prepared against your journey."

Linda reached eagerly for a globe of the crisp

red fruit, but Philip stopped her. She looked up at him, puzzled and angry. "Philip, what's wrong with you? I'm hungry!"

"So am I, but we'll find food outside. Eat nothing here."

Ygerna's voice was soft and dangerous. "And why will you not eat the food of my providing?"

Suddenly Philip felt a courage, even a gaiety, that rose in him from no source he could discover. Boldly he held the witch's gaze. "Because in my world we have a story, which my father told me. There was once a beautiful maiden, whose mother loved her dearly. But the maid was loved also by the Lord of the Dead; and one day while she was picking flowers in a meadow, he stole her and carried her down to his dark kingdom. Her mother grieved and sought for her for many months, and at last found means of rescuing her daughter. But while she was in the underworld, its lord had persuaded her by trickery to eat six pomegranate seeds. And because she had eaten them, the maiden was doomed to spend six months of every year in the Dead Lands with her husband."

"It's not the *same*, Philip!" exclaimed his cousin.

"It is the same. Eat nothing until we are outside."

Linda watched him in astonishment: she had never heard him speak with such authority before. Obediently, she set down the apple. But Ygerna stared at Philip with hatred. Suddenly her hand arched up, as sinuous as a snake; and Philip did not know what spell would have been laid on him if Linda's arm had not shot across his body in a gesture of protection. "Harm him, Sister, and you get no help of me!"

For an instant longer, Ygerna stood in venomous silence. "Very well."

The sound of a horse's whinny came faintly through the trees. "You will ride," said the witch. "Lake Evaine lies westward three days' journey. In your saddlebags you will find a small purse of gold and such food as is suitable for traveling." Her eyes flickered to Philip's face, and in them he saw not only hatred but a swift, fugitive fear. "It may be that very hunger will drive you to eat it. When you come to the lake, you will encounter the Mer-People who inhabit it. Conjure them to help you in our mother's name; they remember still and fear it."

She turned away and bent to unlock a small chest covered with crimson velvet and bound with iron. "They know what you seek and will guide you there. But if you cannot find it—if the golden box has been broken, or the Marrow lost— then you must journey onward to the mountains and seek to buy it from the dwarfs. To that end, I give you this."

She lifted the lid and held up a rope of magnificent tiger-eye jewels. Each was as smooth and heavy as a marble and shimmered with the hues of bronze and honey, while deep in each center shone a twisted core of gold. "They love all gems that have the light of fire caught in them. Show this to their king."

"Perhaps they will take it from us and not give us the Marrow at all," objected Linda.

Ygerna shook her head. "No, they will not steal: they are honorable folk, though grasping and avaricious."

"Suppose we succeed," said Philip. "What then?"

Ygerna spoke urgently. "Then come to me. No, not here! My creatures will bear me through the air; I have strength for one last journey. In Kyril's capital, hard by the walls of his palace, there lies a meadow, and in that meadow stands a ruined tower. It is called the Tower of Orofyn, and men shun it because of an old, sad tale that happened there long ago. There you will find me, either to die or to grow strong again. For if I find new life, I mean to challenge the King in his own city."

Linda's voice was distant and unmoved. "And what shall be our reward, Ygerna?"

"For Philip, return to his own world. For you, whatever you find your heart truly desires: whether to go or stay."

Linda inclined her head in acknowledgement.

Philip glanced at her, troubled and surprised. What had happened to her to replace last night's disbelief with this apparent cold acceptance? "I see we have no choice," she said.

Ygerna's lips widened in a pale smile. "Then you see well. But I do not fear that you will fail me, Linda. Whatever rebellion you may cherish now, your witch-nature will overcome it. It will prove the stronger."

They took no leave of her, but turned away and walked silently to the door. The morning light was barred with the shadows of the trees, and a cool mist coiled in wisps along the ground. Tethered to a branch a few feet away, they found two horses—stolen from where, they could not guess. But they were saddled and heavily laden. The poor beasts were shuddering. Linda went up to one, a mare, and took its muzzle gently between her hands. At once both animals grew quiet and seemed less frightened. "I think they're glad to see a human being," she remarked to Philip.

They mounted. Suddenly the wolf was again waiting for them some way off among the trees. "He will show us the road," said Linda. Philip frowned. How had she known that? Ygerna had not told them.

They followed the wolf. Before long, they came to a track, narrow but clearly marked, that wound away among the overshadowing pines. All at once

Linda drew her mount up and spoke to the shape-shifter. "We thank you for your guidance. But now go back to your mistress and tell her we will have no witch's creature as our companion. Go!"

To Philip's astonishment, the beast turned and vanished among the tree-trunks and did not return.

5

For three days they journeyed through the wilderness. At night they camped on the shore of some small lake, kindling a fire and wrapping themselves in the blankets Ygerna had provided. The track kept close to the water-margin, and so after the first few hours, the forest never again completely hemmed them round.

To Philip, his mind growing more and more deeply silent in the wild stillness that surrounded them, they might almost have been traveling through his own country. In the land he was familiar with, an advancing glacier had scoured thousands of lakes from the rock-basin. He wondered if that had happened in this world as well. Often, as his horse's hoofs crunched and slid softly over some pebble beach, he would gaze down into the water where great boulders, furred with yellow weed, sank to unimaginable depths. They washed their hands and faces in the water and found it very cold.

While they journeyed with Herne, autumn had passed its height: now it was fading into winter. Yellow leaves shriveled to brown and crackled, frail as seashells, underfoot. Philip and Linda slept in the open and woke, cramped with lying upon stones, to see the chill rose of dawn breaking over the water. They saw no living thing except the loons, coasting over the waves in the dawn light, their wings a blur of motion. At that hour and at twilight, the hills echoed with their long, shuddering screams.

And yet Philip knew these lakes were different. Beneath their surface dwelt the Mer-People. He often gazed in puzzlement at the steel-gray water, his mind straining to imagine that life of slime and soundless cold. Then he would shiver with disgust and turn away.

Afterwards he preferred not to remember that journey, for he had never in his life felt so lost and empty of hope. Somehow he would find a way to rescue Linda, even against her will; she *must* come back with him. But as the days passed, and

Linda seemed ever more at home in this strange world, he began to wonder whether the thought of returning had occurred to her, or whether she had deliberately thrust it aside.

"What about your parents?" he said to her one evening, expressing a fear that had troubled him from time to time since the very beginning. "What will they think: that we've run away, been drowned? They'll be terrified."

But Linda merely shrugged. "I expect they'll be all right."

She spoke with complete unconcern. For an instant Philip hated her.

And yet at other times, she had never been so good a companion. Perhaps it was the autumn chill, but her whole body seemed more graceful and more vivid. Black hair, white skin, the rose of lips and cheeks, and the lucent, shifting color of her eyes: suddenly all had slipped into a sharper focus, as though he were seeing her clearly for the first time. Now she often sang as they rode along, her voice challenging the silence; and sometimes she would laugh, a sound strange and sudden as a loon's cry across the water.

But there were certain things she would not speak about. On the second evening, as they sat by their fire, Philip decided that he could bear her secrecy no longer.

They had fed the horses and tethered them

nearby, then hollowed a hearth among the stones. In the highest sky the blue of day still lingered. Later they had eaten their meal: salted meat, fresh bread, and fruit. Philip did not like the food but, after examining it suspiciously on the first day of the journey, had decided it would not harm them. Probably it had been stolen with the horses.

Linda's face glimmered in the spitting firelight. Blue and golden sparks shot up between them. "Linda," said Philip gently, "do you think Ygerna spoke the truth?"

Her head came up. Caution, defensiveness, fear: he saw all these in her stare. "Do you *remember* anything," he pursued, "about—about the things she mentioned?"

She both shook her head and nodded it. The confusion of the gesture struck him with sudden pity. "About my babyhood, you mean. I don't know."

For a moment she was silent. "As Ygerna spoke to me, I seemed to remember a cradle—blue velvet and black velvet—and deep, rich shadows covering the walls. And my mother leaning over me and smiling. She was very beautiful, but cold somehow, and hard." The look of fear intensified. "And she leaned down and picked me up. But that's impossible. I would have been only two weeks old!"

"Perhaps you have a long memory."

She laughed suddenly and leaned back on her

elbows. "If I'm a witch? Perhaps."

Other words framed themselves in Philip's memory: the echo of Herne's voice saying: "Linda, at least, is native to these woods. I have seen forest-people very like to her: my sister is one. When my eyes fell on you, I imagined for an instant that I beheld her, as she was when we were children together."

"Because if it's true," said Philip, "then Herne is your half-brother."

She neither agreed nor denied; her face made no acknowledgement. So in uneasy silence they sat together, and waited for dark to fall.

In the late afternoon of the third day, Philip chanced to glance out across the lake whose shore they were following. He touched Linda's arm. "Look!"

"What?"

"Don't you see something swimming out there?"

"That dark shape? It's an otter."

Philip shook his head. "It's too big."

The sun-glare cast a metallic sheen upon the waves. With the light at its back, they could make out very little of the creature that was swimming out from shore. It moved slowly, keeping level with their horses; and though its face was in shadow, Philip and Linda could feel its thought turned toward them, wondering and wary. "Look, that's the head," said Philip. "You can't see much more above the waves." But even as he spoke, he thought he glimpsed shadowy arms stirring the water: arms whose hands were webbed like the fins of some sea-creature.

For perhaps twenty minutes it followed them. By then the day was rapidly waning, and in the play of light and shadow on the waves, they could not distinguish it for certain. Then suddenly the head sank beneath the water, and they did not see it again.

In the morning of the fourth day, they came to Lake Evaine. Philip had wondered at first how they would know it from the many lesser lakes that surrounded it; but they emerged from a screen of trees and knew at once that they had reached their destination.

It seemed to them like an inland sea, for they could not glimpse the farther shore. Here the wind blew strong and cold across water that was brown in the shallows, but sank to mackerel-silver and then to sapphire, brilliant even under the cool, rain-laden sky.

The pebble-beaches of the other lakes had here become great shelves of rock, sloping down to form basins tangled with lily stems and water-weeds, before dropping into shadow. Even the

trees were taller and of greater girth. All the leaves
had fallen now; only the pine needles hushed and
rustled in the wind.

They rode for a little way without speaking. But
they had not gone far when they came to a ruined
road. It had been skillfully made from blocks of
white stone, and it still wound through the weeds
and the wild grasses; but at the shore it ended with
a pair of blackened columns. Some of the stones
were tumbled and lay in fragments as they had
been shattered. On others, Philip noted the marks
of fire.

"The signs of the King's justice," he murmured.

"So Herne would say," answered his cousin.
"The columns must have stood at the first slope of
a bridge." For, indeed, a few blocks still remained
in place between the pillars, and they sloped upwards at an angle that recreated in Philip's imagi-
nation the strong, springing curve of the arch, its
stones now tumbled and cast down into the shallows.

"Look."

Philip followed the direction of Linda's hand.
Then, at last and in truth, he saw the walls.

Only one ragged spear still reared above the
water: the core of a tower whose facing-blocks had
fallen or been blasted away. The line of the wall
plunged downward into the deep water. Philip felt
awe take hold of him as he thought of the labyrinth

that lay buried beneath the rippling surface.

"It's so silent!" murmured Linda.

Her cousin nodded. "A watching silence."

They dismounted and wandered to the end of the shattered causeway. The water here was not more than five feet deep. Its bed was jagged and tumbled; white stone glimmered beneath the weeds, whose tendrils swayed and streamed in the slow current.

"Well," demanded Philip aloud, "what do we do now?"

At that moment they saw him come, gliding like a great fish through the shallows. The tail was longer than a man's legs and ended in a curved fin; Philip saw the pull and thrust of muscles beneath its smooth brown hide. Amazement and curiosity held him silent. Suddenly he was glad that Ygerna's plots had brought them to this world, if only to see the wonder and strangeness of the Mer-People.

Their observer approached to within three feet of where they stood and drew himself upright in the water, his tail coiled beneath him. From time to time his hands moved, or the fin stirred the water lazily. Only his head, from the chin upward, was raised above the water. At once Philip saw the reason for this: the sides of his neck were layered with pink gills, fine as gauze. They pouted in and out, expelling small jets of water. The eyes, so deep

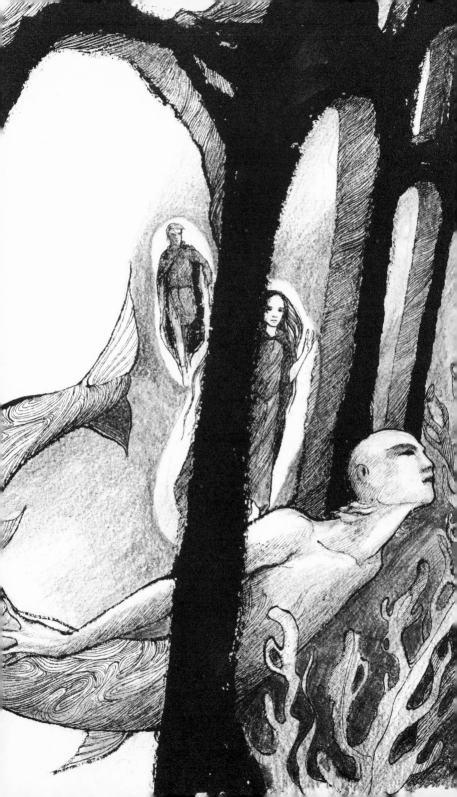

and dark their color could not be guessed, watched the two children intently. But though he felt the acuteness and intelligence of the gaze, Philip realized suddenly that this awareness was alien to his own: it knew no human ways and had no wish to know them.

For a long moment the three watched each other. Then all at once Philip heard words, silent but distinct, form themselves within his mind. "My people have sent me to demand who you may be."

The merman's mouth was rounded, opening and closing in the unaccustomed air. But it had not moved in speech. However, Linda answered without hesitation. Aloud she said, "True names are not to be given lightly. First tell us your own."

"You shall know me by my office," the silent voice replied. "What do you seek? For it is plain that you come to us for service. And indeed the maid resembles another we knew once. We hold her memory in hatred and in fear."

"In the name of that fear, serve us still," commanded Linda. "For Morgan's daughter has sent us on this journey, and her protection is upon us. She still has power to harm you, if you refuse."

Philip turned sharply. "Linda," he whispered, "why do you talk of fear? What harm have they done us? Why should you threaten him?" The merman's gaze flickered to his face.

But Linda gave no sign of having heard. She had

changed. In her, Philip suddenly saw revealed a coldness and strength whose shadow was Ygerna, whose presence he had sensed as Herne spoke of the woman gliding like a ghost among the trees. And all at once he understood his past uneasiness before Linda, his mingling of fascination and dislike. This power had always been latent in her.

In that instant, beyond hope, beyond doubt, he was certain. Linda was a witch: restored to her true world and to her heritage, perhaps a witch more powerful than her dying sister.

And yet, if Herne's father had been the enchanted prisoner who begot her, she was half-human as well. "I will not hate her," thought Philip. "I will not abandon her!" Stifling the panic that rose within him, he forced his attention back to the words that were being spoken.

For a moment he thought he felt a hesitation in the merman's thought, a wavering of fear. At last the silent voice came again. "What do you demand of us?"

"Show us the room that was Morgan's chamber. In it is a golden box and a treasure we have been sent to recover."

"How shall you come with me? You cannot breathe water."

"We won't need to." At last she turned to her cousin. "Philip, I'm going down."

"You're not a strong enough swimmer!"

"Still I'm going. Will you come with me?"

"Of course," he said. Anger and fear for her made his voice harsh. Linda nodded; then, before Philip could move to prevent her, she sat down on the paving-stones and slid, feet first and fully clothed, into the water.

He knew that even here it was above her head. For the fraction of a second pure fear made him hesitate. Linda glided to the bottom, her hair streaming behind her like some strange sea growth, and found her footing on the uneven stones. Then Philip realized that the water was not touching her.

He saw her glance up at him, her face distorted by the waves. But all around her, shielding her, was what looked like a shimmering, transparent silver egg. From time to time, he saw it bend with the current, as though repelling the pressure of the water outside. It was a bubble. Inside it, Linda moved safely and breathed air.

In the despair and amazement of the last few moments, Philip lost all consciousness of fear. Like Linda, he sat and let himself slide downward, his body tensed against the shock of the water's cold. It did not come. All at once a damp, hollow feeling surrounded him; and he too was beneath the waves, looking out through a faintly glistening wall of air.

Linda smiled at him. He could not hear her

thought, but unspoken words of the merman filled his mind. "Very well: I will lead you."

He swam slowly, and they followed, slipping and stumbling over the boulders, which sloped steeply downwards. Trees of weed rose on every side, their fronds bursting into a blossom of light where they drifted upward to the surface. It was by no means a soundless world. Philip could hear the swish and rustle of the waves and the grating whisper of pebbles stirred by the water; and many other sounds came to him indistinctly. Fish darted past them, and here and there a sucking thing clung to a rock. But no fish was as bright as the merman who went before them. As with certain sea creatures, the sun had deadened his brilliance, and it needed the shifting light and shadow of the depths to reveal his skin in its true beauty, a glimmering fluorescence of peacock, lapis, and silver-green.

Enchanted, Philip wandered on, following Linda and their guide. Above him, the surface rippled and pleated in a net of light. He was so absorbed that it seemed a very short time before the bottom leveled out, and they came to the sunken castle, and all brightness was quenched in the water around them.

Philip looked in fear at the shattered walls. Even tumbled and beslimed, the stone blocks were man-high, and the outer wall had been, he guessed, immensely thick. Only an archway now remained. The merman led them through it.

And then they wandered in a maze of corridors and chambers. Tapestries trailed in black slime from the walls. Sometimes their footsteps scraped away the growth and sifting of years, and the fragments of a mosaic glittered beneath their feet, set with garnets and emeralds and squares of blackened silver; or Linda would brush against a doorway, and her hand, grasping for balance, would close on the leering shape of a carven face. Here and there they came upon a chair flung on its side, its legs encrusted with growths of gray anemone; and once, from a shadowed corner, something uncoiled its snake-shape to follow them with its eyes.

At last they came to the smallest room of all. It alone bore signs of having been inhabited. The black posts of a bed, from which some rags of cloth still streamed, were the first thing Philip saw as he drifted through the door a little way behind Linda. Then the dark mouth of a fireplace and a chessboard of jet and ivory, its pale squares cracked and buckled.

Linda's body blocked his full view of the room. She was standing very still, the air-shield wavering and shimmering around her; and even without glimpsing her face, Philip felt her attention riveted on something he could not see. He moved forward and saw what she was gazing at. It must have been made of walnut wood, he thought, dark and shining. Although the boards were swollen with water and their carvings obliterated, he recognized the shape.

It was a cradle.

Near them in the shadows, the merman hovered upright. At last Linda stirred and turned to him. Once again Philip could not hear the question she asked with her mind; but he heard the merman's answer. "Yes, here she lived—she whom we do not name."

A further silence for Philip, which marked a further question from Linda. In answer to it, their guide glided over to a table that stood by one wall. Light fell on it from the decayed and tarnished tracery of a window.

The table was littered with small objects, most of which Philip could not now identify. From their arrangement he guessed that they had been laid out there and sorted through in haste. Linda searched among them with an eagerness that he felt, even though her hands moved with dreamlike slowness, as though weighted by the pressure of the water. She lifted one, and Philip saw it was a casket. She rubbed away the tarnish; through it, Philip glimpsed the color of gold. She worked a moment at the lid and threw it open. The casket was empty.

Slowly, Linda set it down and turned to their guide. Through the shadows Philip saw the merman's smile of triumph. "It is gone, and your search is vain." Again the voice spoke in their inner silence. "Go back to your mistress and give her this message of long hatred. We know that the lesser witch is dying and has no power to harm us. For our sport, we have brought you here. And we will let you return to the upper world alive. Be thankful, and ask no more of us."

Then he was gone, drifting ahead of them. Philip and Linda followed, stumbling and sliding through the drowned chambers, their bodies taut with the fear that, despite his promise, he would abandon them. But he did not, and during the difficult climb up the shore slope, they saw no sign of his kindred.

They emerged on a gravel beach some distance from the road where their mounts were tethered. Their clothes were dry, but Philip's head was aching, both with the strain of fear released and because he had nearly exhausted the air inside the bubble. Above them clouds were moving. The first needles of rain began to fall.

Linda looked at him; her face was bitter and exhausted. She appeared older, thought Philip—almost a woman; and with a pulse of gratitude, he realized that the strangeness and the power had left her. Once again she seemed fully human.

"What shall we do now?" he demanded. "Go back to Ygerna and tell her that we've failed?"

"No." Linda chafed her arms through the gray wool gown. Very softly she added, "Philip, if we did that, I'd be afraid."

"So would I." In the treachery of despair, he felt certain Ygerna would do them what mischief she could; and though she was enfeebled, he knew her to be dangerous. Above all, if he was to rescue Linda and find the counter-spell that would restore them to their own world, they must not turn back.

"Then we bear westward to the mountains." Now where they rose beyond the trees, the peaks seemed no more than distant hillocks, their giant slopes softened by a haze of rain.

Linda nodded. "Ygerna provided for this: we have food for two weeks more."

"Was it she who protected us beneath the water?"

"Who shielded us, you mean? Yes."

"How do you know?"

"She came to me in sleep and told me so."

They did not linger by the burnt pillars. Waves slapped and rippled in the sharpening cold, and the causeway lay melancholy among the rustling grasses. They mounted, drawing their hoods about their faces, and rode away from Lake Evaine.

It was many months before Philip asked Linda what she had imagined or remembered, standing in the witch's bower beside the ruined cradle. But that night as they lay wrapped in their blankets on the ground, she turned her face away and wept, and when he sought to comfort her, she would not tell him why.

6

From that time autumn withered further, and the wind blew cold. Always the mountains loomed before them, drawing nearer day by day, yet always more distant than they seemed.

"How much longer?" Linda would ask.

Philip shrugged. "Perhaps four more days' travel. We're on their first slopes now." Linda looked about them doubtfully and was silent.

Yet Philip could see that the land had begun to rise. Three days out from Lake Evaine, the forest ended and the barrenlands began. Philip and Linda turned back to look one last time at the wall of pine trunks and blue-green needles; then they rode forward. The road could still be followed, though now and then it faded into the grass, and they had to search before rediscovering it some way further on.

They spoke seldom, for their voices jarred the stillness. The bird-calls and water-sounds were left behind, and Philip missed them, chill and desolate though they had sometimes seemed. For miles all around them, the land swelled slowly upwards, sometimes tufting into hillocks, sometimes leveling so the slope could barely be seen. The sky was seldom blue. There were no colors but its pearly light and the turf through which the stony skeleton of the land erupted. They saw no water, though once they came upon the bed of a dry stream. But Linda insisted that there must be water somewhere, for something nourished the matchstick trees that grew thickly in the hollows.

"I wonder who made the path?" said Philip. "We've met no other travelers."

"Yet something made it, and something uses it," answered Linda.

And always the slopes gathered and steepened upward to the mountains. Traveling now in their shadow, Philip could see them clearly. They were tall and yet, he guessed, not so tall as they had once been. Through thousands of centuries their crests had been smoothed by rain and wind, until now they seemed no more than great brown hills. Perhaps, in the chasms he glimpsed in the far distance, there remained peaks as cruel and jagged as they had been in their unremembered morning. But now the slopes seemed gentle: not at all, thought Philip, a proper place for dwarfs.

But, as day followed day, he began to wonder what it was the mountains reminded him of. He sought for the comparison that had been troubling him; after an instant he found it. They reminded him of barrows—the green, sod-covered mounds where slept the ancient dead.

Not for the first time, Philip started from thought and shook himself. He disliked this land —had disliked everything about it since the shape-shifter had led them to the enchanted tree.

Suddenly his mind was silent, recreating in memory the upward sweep of the trunk, the rosy shadows of copper. Why had the walls been sheathed with metal? The question had never occurred to him before.

And just as suddenly he understood the answer: for fear of fire! She must be fallen indeed to dwell in the wilderness, where fire is such a danger. And with the knowledge came an impulse of triumphant laughter. He would remember that there was something Ygerna feared, if ever the need came.

But he suspected enough of what was happening to Linda that he did not tell her his discovery.

Slowly, letting their horses fall to a walking pace, they traveled on.

Linda squinted dubiously at the swift-flowing clouds. "Do you think it's going to rain?"

Anxiety sharpened Philip's voice. "With the country you grew up in, you don't know the look of a snow cloud when you see one? It won't rain."

"We'd best find somewhere sheltered to camp then."

"What do you suggest?" demanded Philip. The surrounding country was flat and bare, even of the small, starved trees. Without waiting for Linda he spurred his horse. "Let's ride on. We've maybe half an hour's light. If we can't find anything in that time, we'll have to choose a hillock on the far side from the wind and make do with that."

Already the storm clouds were deepening toward twilight, and the air was filled with the pungent chill of snow. The first flakes began to fall as the cousins reached agreement and moved on.

But Philip had miscalculated. The snow fell, until at last it seemed they were at the center of a universe of whirling stars, and the light faded quickly. "Are we still on the path?" called Linda above the wind.

Philip shook his head. "I don't know—it's too dark to see!"

As though by consent, they halted. It seemed useless to go on; to do so would be to lose the track, and then who could tell what might befall them? The best thing, thought Philip, would be to camp now when they were still reasonably certain they had not strayed far from the road.

Snowflakes sifted down his collar and settled on his eyelashes. He blinked them away and turned to speak to Linda. In the now nearly total dark, he saw her gazing ahead, her eyes shaded with one hand. "There's a blacker patch—I think there are trees ahead." Philip could see nothing through the swirling dusk, but her sight had always been keener than his own. "And—look, Philip—there's a light!"

It was true. It took him a moment's effort to distinguish it from the thousand snow-stars that obscured his vision, but there it was: a clear, cold point of light.

"A house!" said Linda. "Perhaps they would give us shelter!"

"Wait a minute, Linda. You don't *know* it's a house."

She turned her head impatiently. "What else could it be? Remember, Herne spoke of the forest folk, the woodsmen? We've come upon one of their villages!" And she rode forward at a canter, her mare's hoofs striking down to stone through the snow.

Philip followed with a strange mingling of eagerness and reluctance. He wanted to trust Linda's guess, for the loneliness of their journey had begun to trouble him. It would be good to see other woodsmen like Herne—hunters who perhaps even knew him and could give news of their lost friend. But still some disquiet warned him. He followed Linda, once again cursing the impetuosity that made her despise all caution.

It was not long before he too made out the deeper darkness of the wood. The trees seemed taller than was usual in this barren country and filled the hollow between two hillocks. But to draw close to the light was not so easy. They rode forward, and still it twinkled elusively among the trees.

They came to the outskirts of the wood. Here Linda paused, gazing uncertainly at the slender trunks. Some way ahead, the light shone with a diamond brilliance. Philip came up beside her. "It's a strange place to have a house," she murmured.

It was not until the trees were all around them that they fully realized how strange it was. Straight, thin trunks rayed away into the darkness, cutting off their retreat. The light was very close now. And with the branches clattering and snowflakes drifting downward on the wind, Philip and Linda emerged into a clearing. In its center stood a single tree, and from its lowest branch, a lamp was hanging.

Linda turned to stare at her cousin; he heard her sharp, intaken breath of fear. The rusty handle of the lantern creaked as it swung to and fro.

"Turn around," said Philip quietly. "Let's go back the way we came."

But at that instant he heard Linda scream, and in the same second something struck him on the head and dragged him downwards. There was an explosion of pain, and then darkness overwhelmed him.

7

Philip woke to pain and a hand cupping his head, forcing it upward. "Swallow this. We've waited long enough for you to stir."

A cup was being pressed against his lips. He attempted to fight and spit out the liquid, but despite his resistance he swallowed a little. The shock of the drink brought him back to full awareness.

He was lying on a pallet at the side of a low room. Spaced through the gloom—the light of tallow candles filtered by woodsmoke—he could see the posts that supported the ceiling. To one side stood a divided door, its top half swinging open. From the blackness beyond came the odors of animals, of fodder, and damp earth.

In the center of the main room, a hearth had been sunk into the floor and lined with stones. Its coals smoldered like a bed of garnets, and a pot hung over it, suspended from a hook.

Philip raised his hand, to find that his head had been bandaged. "But—the lantern . . ." he murmured.

The laugh was neither kind nor merry. "The lantern served us well: you were decoyed as others have been before you. But we seldom have such luck in the first weeks of winter."

"Have they anything worth taking?" interrupted a second voice.

"The beasts, the food, some winter garments All will be of use to us."

"But nothing of value?"

"That may be"—a younger voice spoke eagerly —"for they came out of the forest, and I have heard there are strange things hidden there."

"Treasures and powers!" mocked the second voice. "Gareth, treasures do not come to vagabonds like ourselves. Learn that or you'll never make an outlaw."

"Why did we not kill them, then?" The young voice was sullen.

"Because you may be right, Gareth. Cease your quarreling," commanded the first speaker. A hand gripped Philip's shoulder and pulled him upright, dizzy and swaying, on the bed. "Now, Sir Traveler, tell us who you are and where you were going."

Philip saw them standing around him: powerful men and sharp-faced women, all black-haired and black-eyed. Perhaps twelve all told, including the unkempt children whose gaze was as sly and avaricious as their parents'.

By one of the wall-posts Linda was standing, watching him. Her hands had been tied, but otherwise she seemed unharmed.

His head was swiftly clearing; but instinct warned him to feign weakness for a moment longer. "Who are you?" he whispered. "Are you woodsmen?"

Their leader smiled grimly. "Once we were. But I murdered a man, although he was my guest and my sworn friend. For that I was outlawed with all my family. Now we live as best we may: by hunting, trapping, stealing.

"But come," he said: "What is the purpose of your journey?"

"We were traveling toward the mountains." Philip knew he must satisfy them somehow, and between the fear and the pain of his wound, he could not think clearly enough to lie. "We were going to find the dwarfs."

A murmur and an awed, expectant silence. After a moment the outlaw chief spoke again. "The greed of the dwarfs exceeds even their wealth. Anyone who wishes to deal with them must pay a high price. Tell me then: what were you bringing them?"

He looked from Philip's still face to Linda's wary one. "You will not say? We found nothing in your saddle-bags. Perhaps it is something you carry on your persons?" The silence lengthened. "I see I have guessed rightly."

A woman turned to the chieftain and spoke in an angry whisper. Over her drab-colored gown she wore a shawl of red and green; gold bangles glittered at her ears. From her air of assurance, Philip guessed her to be his wife. He nodded and looked consideringly at the prisoners.

The children, too, sensing the hostility of their elders, had grown restless. They began to whisper to each other and to glance at the two captives, their dark eyes glistening with amusement. Philip, hearing the spiteful laughter of boys only a little younger than himself, willed down the anger that threatened to distract him and distort his judgment. He must do something, for he could feel the crowd's attention beginning to turn itself on Linda.

She had remained very quiet with that gift she had for averting notice and punishment. He had seen it often before when she was letting him take the blame for some mischief they had been involved in together. Often, in his first anger over such an episode, he had told himself that she was a sly little coward. But now he saw something more in her face: a subtle wildness, a flickering of danger.

He must distract them from her. But in the instant that he pondered what to do, it was already too late. One of the smaller children, a ragged little girl, her cheeks smeared with soot, ran forward, laughing. Linda's hair hung down over her breast and shoulders. The child seized it in both fists and pulled cruelly.

In that second several things happened. Linda reared back, and her lips parted. Philip heard the sound she made: a soft snarl. The whirling motion tore her hair out of the child's grip and swung a little doeskin bag, which she wore on a cord around her neck, loose from the folds of her gown where it had lain concealed. Ygerna had given it to them, and in it she carried the tiger's-eye necklace.

But for the moment the others saw neither of these things. They heard the snarling noise, almost animal in its savagery, and saw Linda shake herself free. As Linda's eyes lit upon her, the child screamed and fell. Her cry died into nothingness, and silence came.

It was broken by the child's mother, who rushed forward to gather up her daughter. Whatever had happened, the girl seemed to be uninjured, for protected by her mother's arms, she began to wail

and point to Linda. At once a babel broke out. Philip, watching helpless, saw Linda shrink back against the post. The power had flashed out of her like lightning—and then vanished.

"Father! Father!" Suddenly one voice rose above all the others. A young man had entered by the farther door. He was cloaked and hooded, and although he was thinner and darker, Philip recognized him as Gareth's twin. "A party of hunters has been sighted on the road, drawing nearer."

"How many, Jared?" demanded the chieftain.

"Three. They have fat saddlebags and ride unguarded, and they carry lights!"

"Then we shall profit by their foolishness. Come, there is work to do." Already the men and some of the women were in motion: some to saddle horses, others to fetch woolen cloaks and weapons stored in chests against the wall. "Bind the boy. Wulf, you will stay to guard them." Wulf— the man who had spoken mockingly to Gareth— nodded. The outlaw chief turned once more to the prisoners. "And when we return, we will discover what kind of woman can strike a child senseless with her glance. What ails you, Elaine?"—for the girl's mother had come up to him.

"I will not leave my child alone here while *she* remains!" She pointed to Linda.

"Bring her, then, and let the other children come, too, since the road is near. But see they do not hinder us." With that he turned away.

A moment later the two children were alone, except for their guard and a dog that snuffled softly about, nosing for bones among the straw. Faintly outside, they heard the sounds of the out-laws' departure; and Philip experienced an in-stant's pity for the unfortunate travelers who were going to find themselves so far outnumbered.

Then once again there was silence. Wulf squat-ted by the hearth, stirring the coals with a charred stick that lay nearby. He was a lean, ugly man whose cheek had been disfigured by a white knife-scar. Philip and Linda waited.

He threw the stick aside and looked up at her. "Tell me, Mistress, since there is no one but your friend to hear you. Did you make the child fall?"

"I did." Linda spoke softly through the golden gloom. "And I could do the same to you."

"Could you, now? Then the tales of witches are true, it seems." His voice was casual, almost good-natured. As he spoke he reached to one side and took up one of a pile of sticks. Only when he thrust its end among the coals, and the resin-coated tip flared into flame, did Philip realize it was a torch. "But the stories also teach us the remedy."

He straightened and came closer, holding the torch before him. Philip could see the terror be-neath Linda's stillness, and in his helplessness to protect her he heard himself cry out. Wulf glanced at him and grinned. "Do not be afraid. I will not harm her if she keeps still. I will leave her for the others to burn in their good time."

He was standing over Linda now, the torch held near her face. Philip saw her wince away from the flaring heat. "What is it you wear around your neck?" whispered Wulf. "Some treasure that you would not show the others?"

He grasped for the purse—and collapsed without a sound. For an instant Philip thought that Linda had struck him down. Then he saw the smooth, heavy rock that someone had thrown; it had struck Wulf's head and rolled onto the floor.

Someone. But who? The room was empty.

For a moment only. From a trapdoor in the ceiling, a man swung himself down and jumped lightly to the floor. He was small of stature, dressed in leather scarred and weatherstained. "Herne!" cried Philip and Linda together.

Their friend nodded, his swart face creasing in a laugh. "I was hiding in the loft."

"How did you get there?" questioned Linda. Already he had moved to her side and was swiftly cutting through the ropes that bound her.

"With the same cunning that led me to you through the wilderness. But that is a story for the fireside, if fortune favors us and we can travel beyond danger." Linda was now free; Herne turned his attention to her cousin. As his hands were released Philip swayed and with an effort drew himself upright. "You are hurt! Can you walk? We must take to the barrenlands, as far as possible from the road. They have stolen your horses."

Philip nodded uncertainly. "I'll walk because I have to." He must overcome the dizziness; their escape was not yet achieved.

"Let us bind this one, then, and be gone." As Herne knelt to deal with the unconscious guard, Linda ran to the place where their saddlebags lay heaped in a corner. Their contents had been scattered, but not yet carried off.

"There's food," she called quietly, "and here are our cloaks!"

"Put them on, and pack the food in a single bag. There—our friend will not stir till morning."

Swiftly Philip and Linda swung their cloaks across their shoulders. Herne took the loaded saddlebag from her. With no one to see or hear them, they followed him silently out into the dark.

Above them the clearing sky had burst into a bloom of stars. The snow was melting. Another hour and the land would be as bare as though the snowstorm had never swept across it and away into the west.

The outlaws' stronghold lay within the shadow of the wood, but in a few minutes the three fugitives were again on open ground. For Philip, their emergence from the smoke-haze of the stifling room was a relief so great that he felt almost weightless, filled with joy and an irrational confidence. If he had known it, this mood was the product of his wound and of a mounting fever.

It clouded his understanding as well, and it was Linda who first realized the direction in which Herne was leading them. "What are you doing?" she whispered. "You're guiding us *toward* the outlaws—we're moving back the way we came, parallel to the road!"

Herne hushed her with a finger to his lips. "A simple trick, but one they may not expect. I know a place where we can lie hidden. Now be silent until I tell you it is safe to speak."

They followed him, stumbling over the stony ground. Philip did not know how much time passed; no sounds of pursuit came to disturb the dream in which he wandered. Gradually his euphoria faded, and he became aware that he was trembling with weakness, with the sleep that threatened to engulf him. Blood was soaking in a dark stain through the bandage.

He felt Linda's anxious glance. "How much further? They didn't even wash Philip's cut. I think he's ill!"

"Not long now."

No shadow of dawn was in the sky when Herne stopped before a hill-slope, tangled with vines and dead grasses. He lifted them like a curtain, and the children saw the entrance to a cave, no wider than the burrow of a large animal. "Wait," he cautioned them, "until I see that it is safe. Once it was a wolf's lair, but it is long since any creature dwelt here."

They stood in silence. From here the road was hidden from them by the undulations of the land, but its nearness filled them with fear. It was only a moment before Herne emerged from the den and beckoned. Philip knelt to crawl through the opening on his hands and knees. He was through, with Linda following; around him he could see smooth, arching walls and an earthen floor. Then the last of his strength deserted him, and he fell.

He was not unconscious, although faintness prevented him from speaking. He knew when Herne and Linda lifted him and wrapped him round with their cloaks and heard, as though from a great distance, their whispers of anxiety and concern. But in other ways sickness lent a strange clarity to his mind: in the haze that enveloped him he understood one thing Linda herself appeared to have forgotten. This man with whom she was talking so urgently, this man so like her in coloring and stature, was her brother. Philip remembered this and found himself giggling feebly. The others looked at him in fear.

"Can't we give him anything to drink?" demanded Linda.

"We have nothing."

"May we light a fire?"

He shook his head. "We dare not."

So, sitting together among the dank odors of the long-abandoned den, they watched the night away; but the night seemed not to wane. Linda shifted restlessly. "When will the sun rise?"

"Presently. But daylight may bring new danger."

After a moment she said: "Well, there is no fire to cheer us, but tell me your tale. How did you find us? I have not yet thanked you."

Even in the dimness Philip could guess at Herne's twisted smile. "Say nothing of that yet: it is an ill omen to speak thanks too soon. But to wear away the darkness, I will tell you. Following you was easy, once I found you had acquired horses and taken to the road. It was not even difficult to come after you on foot, for you traveled slowly."

Linda nodded. "But how did you escape from the marshes? The carac carried us leagues on down the river!"

"Yes; and I could not possibly have followed you, but for a chance I cannot understand." He halted. When he spoke again, it was with wonder. "I had my knife and did not fear that I would starve. That night I slept on the driest ground that I could find, close by a patch of reeds. And when I woke at daylight, I saw my carac drifting a little way from shore. What power or fortune brought it back to me, I could not tell: not the force that carried you off, I think.

"I determined then to find you. For a day and a night, I let the river carry me into the deep forest, watching always for the faintest traces of your landing on the shore. At last I found them, and with them the prints of the demon-wolf. I followed them, and they led me to a tree."

"A tree?" Linda's voice was wary.

Herne nodded. "It was ancient and rose very high, with a smooth, unbroken trunk. And then, Linda, I saw something so strange that with all my woodcraft I would not believe it. For it was plain that you and Philip had approached the tree and later walked away. But you did not merely go up to it and then turn back. If I believed such things were possible, I would say you went, not up to the tree, but *into* it."

Philip strove to understand, to pierce the weariness that clouded his thoughts. To him, the silence seemed a long one. At last Linda's voice replied: "You saw no door, then. But that was because she chose you should not see. You read the signs rightly, Herne. For hidden in that tree dwells Ygerna, daughter of Morgan."

Philip felt Herne's recoil, and in the gloom saw him sketch a sign: the first and last finger lifted, like a pair of horns. "You have seen her, then," he whispered.

Linda nodded. "We have seen her. She is dying. But she has filled us with the fear of her and set us a task: to bring her the Marrow of the World."

"That is grievous news. Yet I am certain, Linda, that you have not told me the whole of it."

"No, I have not." The darkness between them was tense with that unspoken secret.

"Do you not trust me?" said Herne at last.

Linda shook her head. "I trust you. Oh, Herne, that's not it!"

Philip stirred in his blankets and murmured an incoherent sentence. Herne laid a hand across his forehead. "He burns with fever! If only we had water! But there is no spring within a league of here."

"Would water cool him?"

"Perhaps."

"Then," whispered Linda, "you shall have it."

She turned away. The two men waited: Herne with a fear he could not explain; Philip with the dreaming patience of his sickness.

Suddenly Herne cried out. His hand shot up as though it had been scalded. His fingers were dripping. From the ground beside him, a spring had welled up out of the sand.

It flowed across the dry, gently sloping floor; it was as cold as the depths from which it had come.

Still Herne did not move. *"What are you?"*

Softly and sadly, Linda answered: "I do not know."

She came to Philip then and bathed his forehead, murmuring the ancient, meaningless sounds that women use to comfort a sick child. The coolness soothed him, and he lay quiet. "It's still no good," said Linda. "This alone won't cure him."

Herne, who had moved to the cave's entrance, answered grimly, "Perhaps his cure draws near. Our enemies have found us. Look!"

Linda joined him and carefully drew aside the curtain of dead grass. As she did so, a pearly light filled the cave.

Once again, in the wasteland before them, a lamp was shining.

8

A glowing oval, it seemed to hang suspended in nothingness; it might have been very near them or very far away. Across its surface, like a rainbow in the depths of an opal, there swirled and blended shadows of yellow, green, and rose. Its peaceful light fell through the screen of vines; and even Philip, too dazed to understand, lay serene when the pale glow touched his face.

"It's different," said Linda. "It's not what we saw before! And they wouldn't use the same trick twice—not if they truly wanted to catch us. I think we should go toward it and seek help. We can't go on. Philip needs medicine; he needs sleep!"

"Be careful, Linda! To light a lantern in these parts and let it shine out for all to see, a man must be either wicked or foolish or so powerful he need not fear the guests the lamp may bring him."

"Of your three choices, let us hope the last proves true! If it leads us into danger, then blame me."

"That would give me small comfort," remarked Herne. "Come, help me lift him."

Supporting Philip between them, they approached the light; and it did not draw away into the distance, but loomed before them. Its brilliance was not harsh: they could gaze directly at it and perceive the deeper colors—sparks of ruby and amber, glints of gold—that shimmered in its depths; but it dazzled the darkness around it, plunging the barrenlands into shadow. They could see nothing else; and it was with a curse of astonishment that Herne collided with a low stone wall. Set into it, they saw an open gate.

"This was not here three hours ago," murmured Herne. "We crossed this very ground!"

All at once the air was gentler, as though the wind were the breath of a summer night. They were walking over a deep lawn, and the sweet smell of roses, of grass, and earth pierced Philip's weariness and filled him with strength. He drew himself up and leaned less heavily on Herne's shoulder.

Other odors came to him in strange profusion, some from trees he knew could not possibly grow in this northern country, that seemed to him the fragrance of cedar-oil, of cinnamon, of sandal-wood, and pine. They passed a magnolia bent beneath its load of blossom, each flower as pale as a candle flame, its petals veined with rose; and now and then from some far corner of the garden came the night-song of a bird.

Confidence and peace grew in them as they wandered forward. The suspicion had faded from Herne's face. The globe shone stationary now, shielded from them by a tracery of branches; beyond it rose the white shadow of a building. Softly the three approached.

In the center of the lawn, a man was reading. The stone table at which he sat might have grown out of the earth, for its plinth was crusted deep with moss. He wore a robe of dark green velvet, and around his neck hung a heavy chain, each link formed from a golden rose. A gossamer canopy stretched above him, draped from the branches of two trees: it seemed a fragile shield against the weather. Beside him to light his work, the lamp hung from a pole. Philip thought, "It *can't* have moved—it's been here all the time!"

They made no sound, but still he sensed their presence. He raised his head and looked at them. "Well, my children, so you have come. Yes, Linda, another has said that to you, has she not? But my good will may prove of more use to you than hers."

"Sir," said Linda, "if you know our names, will you not tell us yours?"

Softly he laughed. "Do you think that would be wise? As you yourself have said, true names are not to be given lightly. Yet I will tell you one of mine. I am Leo."

"Who are you," exclaimed Linda, "that know every word we have spoken? I was certain no one heard that, except my cousin and the merman." As she spoke she knelt before him, and because somehow it did not seem courteous to stand in his presence, the other two did likewise.

"You had other hearers, though maybe you did not see them. As for *what* I am, some in their timorousness would call me a wizard. This"—he gestured to the rustling, fragrant shadows of the garden—"is my summer home. I come here sometimes when I wish for solitude. But now the year is dying, and soon it will be time to leave."

Philip, his weariness banished with his fear, gazed at Leo's face. All its lines swept upward, from the black brows to the corners of the thin, laughing mouth. His skin was very dark. Beneath their lids his eyes were green as emerald. Kindness, sternness, and nobility all were written in the face, together with a quality of common shrewdness that disconcerted Philip and made him lower his eyes.

"Do not kneel before me. Come here, Linda." As the others got to their feet she went forward. Leo took her face between his hands. Philip felt the depth of his gaze, but Linda met it proudly, although her expression grew wary.

At last Leo stirred and nodded. As though speaking only to her, he said, "You are burdened, and with a choice not wholly of your seeking. Rest here, and be at peace for a while." He swept his thumbs gently down across her eyelids, and beneath their pressure Philip saw the tension ease from his cousin's face.

Leo released her. "Welcome, Herne, the King's good huntsman."

"The King's, sir? He knows nothing of me."

But Leo only smiled. "Philip, you are hurt."

The dizziness was returning, and the lightness in his head made speech come quick and easy. "Please, sir, there are three travelers on the road. We believe the outlaws have attacked them. Can you not do something to help?"

Leo rose; they saw that he was very tall. "Such generous thoughts should be rewarded. But the travelers have taken no harm. They were only bait and were closely followed by a company of King Kyril's guard. By now the outlaws have been captured and will be brought before a court. The women and children will be treated mercifully, and such of the men as wish to follow an honest trade will be given the means to do so. But come in; clean beds await you, fresh linen, and hot water. Philip, I will look to your wound."

After that Philip remembered whitewashed walls and floors of honey-colored wood, a bed with plain varnished posts, and a coverlet of velvet. He remembered a sense of cleanliness, as gentle hands stripped away the old bandage, washed his wound and anointed it with a soothing salve. With all these impressions flowing confusedly through his mind, he tumbled into sleep.

In that house they were healed. Hours blended into days, with music and talk and quiet occupations. They saw no servants, but twice each day a meal awaited them in a room floored with squares of dark blue stone—in the morning, bread, honey, milk, and cheese; in the evening, fruit, stewed meats, and cinnamon-creams in cups of almond paste. They ate from wooden plates, but Leo's own goblet was a silver-gilt rooster, its body formed of a polished cocoanut-shell.

Except for their host, who spent many hours of each day alone, they saw no living thing but Leo's birds. Some there were whose feathers shimmered with lapis and golden-green; others whose plumage had the color and softness of old velvet; and plain little sparrows whom their master seemed to cherish as much as any. Linda would sit in patient stillness, waiting for a bird to alight in her outstretched hand or coax it to take a kernel of grain from between her lips.

In Leo's garden summer lingered. Here and there a petal was curling into brown, or a leaf was webbed with scarlet veins. But Philip suspected that however thickly the snow had blown on the night they followed the outlaws' lantern, it had not fallen here.

Leo they seldom saw. When he did appear, it was usually in the evening, and then he played to them on an instrument that resembled a small harp or talked about his creatures and their ways. But he would answer few of their questions and none about himself.

Afterwards, remembering, Philip found that his dominant impression of that time was silence—Herne's contented stillness, for in Leo's house he had become oddly shy and gentle; Linda's reserve, more enigmatic than ever. Philip did not know what she was thinking, and she did not confide in him; he knew that Leo's knowledge of their past had impressed and frightened her. Sometimes she would look fretful, sometimes sad; but at moments her care would vanish, and she would laugh with a gaiety and gentleness Philip had never seen in her in the old days. As for Philip, the exhilaration of returning health filled him with calm delight.

One evening Leo summoned them to a room they had never seen before. The ceiling rose above them, curved like an inverted bowl. It was painted black.

"I have something to show you," said Leo, "for your good or your amusement, whichever you may choose. Our time together is drawing to an end; for you have an errand still unfinished, and tomorrow I must send you on your way."

He quenched the candle flame; his voice, quiet, magical, continued speaking out of the darkness. "We will visit Philip's world: a journey I have never made, save by this means. Watch now."

Philip leaned back in his chair, gazing upwards where he knew the black dome to be. Herne's fingers closed over his, gripping them for one sharp instant, and in that pressure he felt the question, "*Your* world?"

But then he forgot Herne; for suddenly the dark was night, the air around was the still, hot air of summer. "We will visit the Land Between the Two Rivers," whispered Leo's voice, "and the ancient city of Agade, when Sargon was its king."

Stars were pricking out of the blackness above their heads—first palely, then with greater brightness, until they shone like ice crystals, brilliant and remote. In their dim light Philip could see a plain spread before him, inlaid with fields and crisscrossed by canals; and far on the horizon, the great piled ziggurat that men had built to imitate the Sacred Mountain. All lay still beneath the summer heat of a night four thousand years ago.

He closed his eyes. Like the pulsing of his own blood, he could feel the dark mass of the earth in its orbit around the sun. Then, by degrees so slow the eye could hardly see them, another planet rose above the ancient plain. At the sight of it, Philip's thought cried out in recognition and worship far older than the body in which he dwelt. Venus, Isis, Ashtaroth, Inanna!

The vision faded. For a moment all was gray. Then once again stars bloomed, and this time they were stars he knew, configurations he had often traced in the winter sky. It was his own countryside; he could see the ragged peaks of elms and crusted snow that sparkled like gold and silver dust. And high in the black dome, the Northern Lights were glimmering as he had sometimes stood sleepless to see them, impatient of the cold—pale sheets of green and rose, unfolding, furling, fading.

"And now a time no one will ever see." Leo spoke, and the familiar countryside faded into shadow at his words. "For the souls of men will have fled to other worlds, and no eyes will watch the dying of the sun." Then it seemed to Philip that he saw a wasteland where oceans and peaks of ice shone dully in the glow of a vast red sun.

"Leo, enough! No more, I beg you!" The voice was Linda's.

The room faded to shadow; then suddenly it was the house they knew, and the candle was burning on the table. Leo gazed at Linda, and she stared back at him. Her face was haggard with astonished accusation.

"Linda," said Leo softly, "which of these worlds is your home—here or there?"

"I do not know!"

She shook her head with such violence that the black hair whipped against her cheeks. But Leo, grasping her wrists, pulled her down onto her knees beside him. "Linda, which one?"

"I don't *know!*"

To Philip, it seemed that her face was contorted, not by grief, but by furious anger; a single tear slid from beneath her tightly closed lids and down into her mouth.

Leo's face grew less harsh. He touched the tear as though it were some rare jewel and then with care and gentleness wiped it away. "In your heart I think that you already know."

He caught her among the white-marble shadows of a colonnade. "Linda!"

"Yes?"

"May I speak to you?"

She paused, her whole body tensed for flight.

"That depends on what you want to say."

"Leo says we must leave tomorrow. I had to talk to you before then."

"What about?"

"Linda, I'm uneasy."

She gave no sign of interest or concern, only stared at him calmly. "Why?"

"Because we're following a path marked out for us."

Linda looked away. Philip laid a hand on her shoulder, but she turned from him with the abruptness of a whip-crack and stood gazing out into the flower-scented darkness of the garden.

"Doesn't it trouble you, too—that we're only following Ygerna's orders?"

"No, it does not trouble me. What else can we do?"

"Strike out on our own! We are no better than her creatures, as long as we do only what she orders us! How can we hope to defeat her if she is able to follow us so closely?"

"Defeat her." Linda spoke softly, as though considering the words. "We must *not* defeat her. Only she can lift the spell."

"No! There is another, Linda: the King!"

She turned, astonishment in her face. Philip was so absorbed in what he was saying that he did not see her amazement change into fury. "I first thought of it when my wound began to heal. I lay there, remembering all we had said and done. What Leo told us about the capture of the outlaws came back to me: how, even here in the wilderness, the King is watchful and his vengeance swift. Kyril is a wizard: it was he who banished Morgan. We must seek him out. I am certain he can help us!"

Only now did Philip glance at Linda.

Gazing up at him was a face transformed: Linda's child-features had hardened into a mask of willful cruelty and power. Philip swore softly and stepped back. He had never seen the witch in her so nakedly displayed.

"We will follow the path marked out." Her tone made this an order he could not disobey; her voice might have been Ygerna's own. "This is not only my sister's choice, but mine. Do you understand, Philip? *I* choose it."

He could feel her power commanding, compelling him; his mind strained against it with silent resistance. So real was the contest that it was a long moment before he realized he had not answered in words. "What if I refuse to come with you?"

"I could make you, of course."

He forced all his hatred of the power that possessed her into the soft contempt of his reply. "And will you?"

She hesitated. The witch half of her flickered, and for a bare instant Linda's other self gazed out at him through her eyes, the eyes of a young girl, filled with fear and loneliness.

But even as he cried out in pity, the power was back in its full strength, and her gentleness was transformed into hatred. She gave him one look, and, turning, walked swiftly away down the corridor.

9

Five days later, on an autumn afternoon of chill
sunlight, three travelers rode up to the great gate
of the Dwarf Kingdom. Once beyond the barrenlands, they had had no doubt of their road: the
dwarfish highway ran before them to the very foot
of the mountain. There, twisting and looping back
upon itself, it began the steep climb upward to the
gates.

The travelers themselves awakened some doubt
in the mind of the door-warden. He did not fear
them, for only one was a warrior, the others a boy
and a girl. The man and the boy were simply but
richly dressed in robes of blue and gray, with black

cloaks thrown back over their shoulders; but their garments were belted and buckled with gold. The maiden wore a gown of black, high-throated and tight-sleeved; a grass-green cloak billowed out from her body in the wind. All three led horses whose saddles were made of silver and tooled leather. They had taken leave of Leo with affectionate gratitude; all these things had been his gifts to them at parting.

To Philip, his first sight of the dwarf-people was strange and wonderful. Above them rose the gate into the mountain, with its doors of brass and its pillars of twisted stone. Thirty dwarfs, the door-guards, flanked it on either side; and Philip saw that they carried not swords, not even battle-axes, but picks such as miners might use for hewing stone. These picks were no homely tools, but weapons—their curved heads made of iron, their handles gilded and intricately carved.

The door-warden, a dwarf whose beard was braided and tucked into his belt, stood no higher than Philip's shoulder; but Philip saw the square, powerful body, and knew the dwarf was many times his match in strength. He measured the three travelers; his face was grim and shrewd. "I am Helve, dwarf of the Stone People, Warden of the Eastern Door. Before I can give you leave to pass, I must know your business, friends."

"We come to buy," said Linda, "and in payment we are prepared to offer a rich gift."

"What service do you seek?"

"That is a matter so secret we will tell it only to your king."

Helve grunted. "Well, we trade in such things: meat and grain in exchange for our jewels, wood and fine cloth as a just price for our skill in metal-work. It is our livelihood. The Lord Barkhan holds audience at"—he grimaced, and squinted at the sky—"what you men would call the hour of sun-set. Your beasts will be lodged and yourselves hon-orably entertained till then. Let them pass!"

The doors swung silently back; Herne, Philip, and Linda rode into the dwarf-kingdom. Before them, the highway stretched into unguessed dis-tance; for it bored a straight path through the mountain, until it opened at last on the Western Stairs that looked out over the downs.

On and on went the road, and the torches that lit it were like two necklaces of gems, diminishing into darkness. Far above them arched the roof, but the walls were smooth. Lesser roads opened to right and left, and from them came the glow of lights, and the multitudinous echoes of footsteps and of voices. Many dwarfs were walking down the highway—some in stained leather tunics as though they had just come from the mines, others dressed in velvet got by trade and loaded with the rings and enameled chains they loved to wear. But they saw no other riders.

Linda had taken it on herself to be their leader from the moment they spoke with Helve. Now she rode on before her two companions. In front of him, Philip could see her small, proud head, her narrow shoulders softened by the folds of the cloak. Her hair, as rich and heavy as black silk, hung down and brushed the saddle.

Herne's sudden whisper was too low for her to hear. "Why do I help you? This is an evil errand!"

"I know." Philip too spoke softly. It saddened him to know that, in this sense at least, Linda was their enemy and must not overhear. "Herne, I thought much about this when we were in Leo's house. I have no desire to restore Ygerna to life or to kill the King, as I'm afraid she means to do. But whatever we do in the end, our road lies forward."

"Why? What help can we hope to find at the end of this quest?"

"Our hope lies in King Kyril!"

Herne was watching him intently, understanding in his eyes. At that instant Linda turned. Perhaps she had caught some echo of their voices. Her pale face, framed by its veil of hair, suddenly bore so strong a resemblance to Ygerna's that Philip felt his body tighten in alarm.

When they had gone a little way, a dwarf named Horn came forward and introduced himself as their appointed guide. It was his duty to stable their horses and conduct them to the chamber that was to be theirs during the hours before the audience. It opened off one of the narrower streets, whose walls were lined with many similar doors. Horn left them with the promise of a meal and went off to order it.

In all the room there was no visible source of light, no air, no unencumbered space. Colors glowed in dark magnificence from the tapestries, from the ceiling painted with purple and embossed with gold, from the carpet as deep as a moss-grown lawn. Each chair was of carven wood, so heavy that Linda could not have lifted one with all her strength. Emerald and ebony, scarlet and vermilion: the three companions contemplated this richness in oppressive silence.

The meal was brought and did a little to cheer them, for though they carried fresh supplies of food, they had grown tired of travelers' fare. It seemed to Philip that everything was spiced: the baked meat, the wine that the dwarf-servants poured hot into wooden goblets, the orange slices crusted with sugar, cinnamon, and cloves. Still he found the food delicious and excellently cooked.

In the hours of waiting that remained, they talked a little and listened as Linda played the harp that had been left for their amusement. She had first attempted to play only a week before at Leo's urging; but her skill did not surprise Philip. Very little that had to do with his cousin surprised him any more.

When the sun was setting in the world outside and the Eastern Gate was plunged in shadow, Horn led them to the Lord Barkhan's audience chamber. He was not called a king, for the dwarfs were too proud to suffer such a title or to let themselves be ruled, save by one whom they knew to be more cunning than themselves. Cunning, indeed, Barkhan's face revealed, and a cynicism that seemed strange, for as a rule his kindred were grasping but trustworthy. Philip guessed that Barkhan lacked something of their harsh integrity.

Before leaving their own quarters, Linda had drawn the tiger's-eye necklace from its hiding-place and clasped it around her throat. Against the somber color of her gown the stones were so magnificent that even their guide could not help turning covertly from time to time to stare. But Linda had walked proudly on, as if to say that such jewels were merely trinkets for the dwarfs to gaze at with wonder and envy if they chose.

Barkhan's chamber was lit by torches and crowded with many of his folk. The Lord of the Stone People sat on a throne fashioned from three stalagmites, still rooted in the rock where they had grown: a small one at each side, and one great

spear forming the back of his chair. Around this skeleton the dwarfs had woven a web of filigree, whose threads were twisted from white and yellow gold; they had set a seat there and studded it with bloodstone, beryl, and aquamarine.

Barkhan himself awaited them. Sewn to his crimson gown were topazes—hundreds of them—that winked and shone in the pale light. But none was so fine as the stones around Linda's throat, and many eyes were on them as the three advanced slowly the length of the hall.

From the roof above Barkhan's throne, stalactites hung in a toothed curtain, and from the floor stalagmites rose: some as frail to all seeming as icicles, to be snapped with a pressure of the hand; some tall as spears; others that had frozen into pillars thick as trees, reaching from roof to floor. At first glance all appeared to be milky white. But when Philip looked more closely he saw that colors glowed in the translucence of the stone: now yellow, now ice-green, now lilac, or palest orange. "They almost have the glow of living flesh!" he exclaimed.

"And why not?" demanded Horn. "For stone is living, though to men who flourish and die as swiftly as the grass, it may not seem so."

They had now reached Barkhan's throne and knelt before it. "Hail, Lord of the Stone People!" they said in unison.

127

Barkhan raised his hand in greeting. "Welcome to our guests, who have come out of the wilderness with a petition and, I hear, with a rich gift." His words were for them, but his eyes were on the necklace. Helve, relieved of his duties at the gate, stood at his right hand. "What would you have of us?"

"My lord, we seek the Marrow and come prepared to buy it."

There was a murmur of amazement and uneasiness. Barkhan silenced it with a gesture. "Who seeks the Marrow, Mistress? It is the fate of all men to die."

"Some there are, my lord, who cannot resign themselves to death. But you know well that no *man* has sent us." Linda's voice was carefully respectful, despite the arrogance of her words.

Barkhan shifted, and his broad hand gripped the arm of his chair. "You wish to obtain how much?"

"Only a little: as much as may fill this box." And Linda held up the carven sandalwood box that Ygerna had placed in her saddlebag on the day they set out toward Lake Evaine.

Barkhan gave a short, hard snort of laughter. "Just so much as may restore a witch's life! Oh, yes, we hear the news in these parts, for all you may think we spend our lives burrowing like moles beneath the ground. But the sorceress had some hidden in her chamber. Have you searched among the ruins?"

"Yes, Lord Barkhan. It was gone."

He gave a scornful smile. "So the Mer-People despoiled her palace when the fear of her no longer kept them from it? Well, they are a cowardly folk, and that we have always known."

"My lord!" interrupted Helve. "We must not give them what they ask—no matter what they offer us in payment."

"Why not, Helve?"

"The Marrow is a great gift: the greatest, perhaps, the dwarfs can give to mortal men, though for all the harm it has done, I wish it were buried and forgotten. And it has never yet been used except for evil."

Barkhan turned again to Linda. "What would you bribe us with?"

In silence she unclasped the necklace and held it up. The stones shimmered with bronze and honey, and deep in each the torchlight caught a twisted core of gold.

Barkhan leaned forward. Almost against his will a soft, gloating sound escaped him, a murmur of covetousness. "Well, you shall have what you ask. No, be at peace, Helve! Let them bring the book."

A parchment book was brought, bound in red leather. "You will leave the necklace with the jewel-warden, and your deposit will be recorded. He will hold it safe until you return with the Marrow, for we will not claim our fee until the service has been successfully performed."

"I would prefer, my lord, to guard the necklace myself until that time."

"That cannot be. We are no thieves, Mistress, and never in our long history have we proven ungenerous to guests—save now and then, when they came not with friendship but with treachery. Give him the necklace."

Reluctantly Linda rendered up the necklace to the jewel-warden, who locked it in an iron chest. "When may we start?"

"When Ninhirga rises. She is our protectress, and her sign in the night sky is the Emerald Star. Such enterprises should begin at an auspicious moment. You have perhaps three hours to wait. You will go alone, since you act as spokesman for your friends, and Helve will be your guide."

Four voices cried out: Helve in protest, Linda, Herne, and Philip in indignant dismay. "Alone?" exclaimed Linda. "What of my companions?"

"They will await your return. You must walk blindfolded until it is certain you cannot memorize the way. No, say no more!"

His sudden shout was so terrible that it quelled them. Barkhan lowered his clenched fist in token of dismissal. "I have commanded it; it is sufficient."

"Very well." Helve spoke in the darkness beside her. "You may untie the blindfold."

Linda reached up and, with trembling fingers, unknotted the strip of cloth that bound her eyes. But blackness still surrounded her, blackness so profound she could not even see the hand she raised to reassure herself that her eyes were truly open. The terror of blindness seized her. "It's dark! Helve, I can't see!"

"Do not be afraid." To judge by the sounds he must be very near; but the dark was as cavernous as though she had been alone. "Dwarfs need no light to walk on pathways that they know. Take my hand. A little further on, the way is lit."

His broad, hard fingers closed around her own. With that contact Linda felt her courage returning. Helve drew her on, guiding her through the night below the earth.

They were now so deep into the mountain that Linda could never have found the way back, could not even remember the twists and turnings by which they had come. She had left Herne and Philip, full of fear for her and of anger at their own exclusion, and walked with Helve along the stone highway. Then they had turned into a sidestreet, from which a path sloped downward to a guarded door. There the kerchief had been tied around her face, and the door swung shut behind them. After that she knew only that sometimes there were walls, rough-cut and slimed with seeping water, that she touched with groping hands; and some-times corridors where their footsteps echoed and the air smelled cool and stale. Now and again the rock sloped downward beneath her feet, or they came to a step down which Helve handed her carefully. But ever, as they went deeper, the air grew closer and hotter, like the breath of some great beast crouching in the darkness.

If Helve abandoned her or lost the way, she knew that she would die here, for never could she retrace the maze that had brought them to where they stood. It took all the courage of which she was capable (and that was a great deal) to go forward without shaking or allowing her wits to grow blunt with fear.

In the pit-blackness they saw the glimmering when it was still a half-mile distant. With many slow steps they drew nearer to it; and at last they emerged into a cavern. Here and there, at long in-tervals, torches shed their ivory-pale light in a sad illumination; but even that seemed good to Linda's eyes. Helve looked at her with a faint, grim smile. "Yes, even my heart rejoices at the light on such a road as this."

She looked around. "What is this?" She spoke quietly, but her words multiplied in short, muf-fled echoes, shuddering through an air that no sound had stirred for perhaps more than a century. "Why are the walls concave? It's like being inside

a giant barrel. And those are the barrel-hoops!"
She pointed to the curved sweeps of stone, each as
smooth and thick as a tree trunk, that barred the
faintly glittering walls.

Her eyes, dark with awe, returned to the face of
her guide. "But they aren't barrel-hoops, are they?"

"No." Helve shook his head. "They are bones."

And now Linda saw that indeed they stood inside a cage of ribs. Each bone, shining umber with
the minerals that had impregnated it, swept upward to the giant spine that formed the roof-tree
of the cave. How many ages had passed since this
leviathan had drifted to the floor of some forgotten
sea? Long enough for rock to have hardened from
the sand that sifted through his bones. "In my
world," she whispered, "we tell a story about a
man who was swallowed by a whale."

"I do not envy him!" Helve spoke shortly, but in
his face she saw mirrored her own astonished rev-
erence. He took her hand. In that age-old silence,
the touch comforted them both. "Come now."

They wandered on, past the eye-sockets now
blind with stone, through the great jaws. Some of
the teeth were shattered, some still wickedly
curved and as thick as Linda's fist. Then the mon-
ster was forgotten. Linda halted and gave a soft
cry.

For the cavern looked down on a great plain.
The roof hung low above it, but she could see no

end, no further shore. At their feet endless steps plunged downward, between walls hewn by dwarfish axes. Helve pointed. "That is the bed of the first ocean. Long ago the waters sank, and the earth closed round it." Suddenly, in a voice that rang between the walls, he exclaimed:

"Praised be Ninhirga, the Mother of all wonders! Into all creatures she breathes the breath of life. She gives, and she takes away. May she cleanse us of the crime of profanation!"

At his cry, all Linda's strength deserted her: her legs gave way, and she collapsed upon the ground. For a moment she sat there, her knees huddled against her chin, striving to master her terror. "Helve, we should not meddle with these ancient things!"

He nodded gravely and gave his hand to help her to her feet. "If these caverns were sealed forever, I should be content. For here we behold the desolation to which all things must come. It is best to be happy within the bounds of our small lives, and bless that blindness and be wise."

Two tiny figures in that enormous silence, they began to descend the steps. In the deep-cut walls, their secrets exposed to view, the tale of ages lay revealed. Here and there the stone was embossed with shells. Farther down Linda saw the bones of a great creature splayed in death, a frozen writhing of fins, swan-neck, and slender tail. Lower still, the trunks of trees were embedded, their bark scaled and stippled like the hides of animals; and above them, traced smoke-like in the rock, the fronds of ancient palms.

At last the steps were past, and they emerged onto the seabed. In all the world there seemed to be no sound; even echoes died beneath the stone ceiling. They walked past boulders, over beds of crystal and white gravel, across wastes of seamed and sun-cracked mud—though it was long, Linda knew, since the sun had shone here. The entire plain was lit by the faint glow of torches; but this sign of living presence seemed more desolate even than the piles of clattering shells or the half-buried bones that glittered from the ground.

Now Linda could not control her trembling or the fear that they had indeed profaned a mystery. She lost all awareness of the time in which they journeyed, bearing always toward a fissure that opened some way before them.

At last they stood upon its edge. It plunged down perhaps five meters; a ladder had been set there.

Helve pointed to it. "At the bottom you will find the Marrow: gather it into your box. Go down, and I will wait."

"You will leave me!" In her panic she clung to him. "You will take the ladder and leave me!"

"Mistress, I am an honorable dwarf, no murderer. I would not leave anyone to die here, were he the one I hated most on the earth or under it. I will wait for you as I promised. But I will not touch the Marrow."

For a long moment she looked at him. Something in his gaze reassured her, for at last she nodded. "Forgive me for my cowardice. I will go down."

The ladder was old and shook beneath her weight. She passed stripes of black sand and beds of layered shells, climbing always down into the heat and the rich, dark smell. At last she stood upon firm ground. She knelt and laid her palms against the Marrow of the World.

Its texture was that of moist, heavy earth; but its color was indigo. All the blue Linda had ever seen seemed concentrated there: the brilliance of the peacock, the kingfisher, the sapphire, the fire-opal. Scrabbling hastily, she filled Ygerna's box, and the Marrow caked beneath her nails. Vague memories of its virtue and the purpose for which Ygerna needed it passed through her mind.

She glanced stealthily up at Helve. His head was turned away. She took a grain of the Marrow and placed it upon her tongue. Its taste reminded her of dark, deep things: of damp earth, of mould and stones, and dust laid by the rain. She swallowed. And for that reason, she lived to a great age.

Never afterwards could Linda remember the journey back. Her mind was void, her body heavy with exhaustion. The steps, the walls, the cavern of bones, the darkness, the iron door; then an explosion of light and color that was their room. People were moving about her—she heard the voices of her companions, but what they said she did not understand. She found her way stumblingly to the bed and fell instantly into a dreamless sleep.

10

"Linda is tired." Herne gestured toward the slender figure, head hanging, shoulders slumped with weariness, that rode a little way behind them.

Philip nodded. "I know. She's been that way ever since she came back with Helve. I wish she'd tell us what she saw down there."

The sun was setting among swiftly-flowing clouds. Philip had never seen anything to compare with them: three banks of cloud were converging from north, south, and east, drifting along the sky like mountain-ranges. the oblique sunset rays turned the smoky peaks to red and orange; great shadows fell upon the land beneath.

"We cannot camp tonight," Herne said, scanning the stormy sky.

Philip nodded. "No, we must seek shelter. Look —on top of that rise! Isn't that a farmhouse?"

Two days had passed since they had bidden farewell to Barkhan, well-satisfied with his prize, and Linda had parted from Helve with the mute understanding of those who have shared an experience that cannot be told in words. Once past the Western Stairs, which marked the boundary of the dwarf-kingdom, they drew near to the most peopled area of King Kyril's land. At first they saw only woodlands, hills, and meadows filled with grasses and wild grain. It was rough country, but fertile and pleasant to eyes wearied of the wilderness. Here and there they came upon tilled earth and small houses built of gray country stone. But these homesteads had an air of melancholy isolation, and did not tempt the travelers to seek either company or shelter.

In the storm that threatened, however, only a roof could keep them safe and dry. "Let's ride up to the door," suggested Philip. "Surely they will not deny us hospitality, strangers though we are. And we still have some of Ygerna's gold to pay them for their trouble."

He and Herne turned their mounts toward the path that led up the hill. Listlessly, Linda followed.

As they climbed higher and the house came

into view, a feeling of uneasiness began to grow in Philip's mind. Grass grew between the cobbles of the path. He saw no fresh-turned earth, no animals; the only sound was a distant rumbling from the place, miles away, where the storm had already broken.

They rode into the courtyard. Still no one came out to greet them. The yard itself formed three sides of a square. Before them rose the house, its windows dark as a blind man's eyes, its stone walls desolate in the gray light. On either side stood wooden outbuildings, their roofs thatched with straw.

"It looks deserted."

"If so, then recently," Herne replied. "Look—a sickle lies there on the ground, and its blade is hardly rusted."

"Why would they have left, I wonder?" murmured Philip.

"Do you mean to stay here?" asked Linda.

"If we can force our way in. Why, don't you like the place?"

She did not answer, only gazed around at the deserted buildings. Her look of indifference had disappeared, to be replaced by a frown of troubled uncertainty.

"The stable-door stands open," said Herne. "I'll lead the horses in and tend them, while you search out a place for us to shelter."

Philip nodded. As he did so, lightning split the sky with its jagged brilliance. A moment's quiet— then the thunder burst above them, pealing and tumbling overhead like stone pins scattered by a giant's bowling-ball. Involuntarily, they flinched and pressed their hands against their ears.

When he could make himself heard again, Philip exclaimed: "Look, there's a cellar door! If it's dry, we'll make do with it. There's no time to waste breaking into the house."

He pointed to a square, stone-cut door, half sunk below ground-level and reached by three shallow steps. Only blackness showed beyond it. Pulling Linda after him, Philip hurried forward, while Herne led the horses to what had once been the stable.

A flight of stairs led down. Rough stone met Linda's fingers. "Philip, I don't like it here: it has a nasty *feel*."

The words seemed to whisper in the shadows below them. For a moment they stood silent, listening to the faint sounds. Reluctantly Linda followed her cousin down the steep-cut steps. But all too soon the stairway ended, and they emerged on a large room.

It was certainly a cellar; once, Philip guessed, it had been used for storage. The floor was bare, with an almost polished smoothness; the walls were made of great blocks fitted close together.

High up, three windows shed a stormy evening light. On the floor lay a heap of rags.

The air was dry and cool. Philip was just drawing breath to express his satisfaction when Linda said, suddenly and with absolute conviction, "This house is haunted."

"What? Linda, don't be stupid! You've been starting at every shadow since you came back with Helve from that adventure you won't tell us anything about."

She was not listening. Instead she was gazing with hungry intentness into the dim, silent room.

"Linda—!" began Philip again.

At that instant three things happened. He became aware of hasty steps on the stairs behind them. Linda cried: "Herne, stay where you are!" Herne, startled by the abruptness and urgency of the command, hesitated in the doorway.

And then the pile of rags began to move.

It stirred and seemed to swell a little, and became a crouched body. Moving silently in the gloom, it unfolded like a chrysalis, and grew to the stature of a child. Falling over its shoulders, Philip could see a sheaf of golden hair.

"It's a little girl!" He whispered it, plucking at Linda's sleeve. "See, it's only a child hiding, playing a trick, a game!"

So intent was she that she could not spare him

even contempt. "Then what terrorized the family? Why is the house abandoned?"

Silent, self-absorbed, the shadowy body continued its growing and unfolding. Two small hands, two thin arms white as bone, were stretched above its head: the fingers fluttered. The gesture bore a brief, comical resemblance to someone stretching himself after sleep. But something in those small curved fingers caused Philip to shrink back, made still by sudden doubt.

Then the child turned toward them, searching the gloom where it knew they were standing. It had indeed the stature of a young girl, but Philip no longer thought of *she*, only of *it*. The apparition's mouth was fixed in a frozen smile. Its eyes watched them slyly from the shadows of its hair.

It came toward them, its little hands outstretched, pleading, beckoning. Its smile was ravenous.

And then Linda stepped forth to meet it.

With a heartbeat of fear and gratitude, Philip knew that she was doing this to shield them, himself and Herne, from the evil that—rising from its own place, summoned by who knew what chance word or deliberate incantation—had taken this house for its own.

He watched the two draw near each other, Linda and the opponent who might prove to be her equal. Both wore the appearance of young girls: neither was what she seemed. Linda, human still, though

wasting into an ever stronger resemblance to Ygerna's haggard beauty; the other, a travesty of a child, decked all in garish color: the skin too white, the lips too red, the hair too bright a gold. The creature's hands reached out; Philip saw that the nails were claws.

They circled slowly, holding a constant distance. "She cannot win—it is too strong for her," thought Philip. And indeed in that small figure, incongruous with its marigold hair, its claws, and frozen smile, he sensed a concentrated evil as far beyond his experience as it was beyond his strength to endure.

Suddenly Linda straightened, as if some alien power had filled her body. Her face altered, the mask of Ygerna superimposed upon her own. Her voice keened upward in a terrible sound, part scream of despair, part battle-cry, and she sprang forward, tearing at the demon with her hands. Her nails swept through the flesh as though it had been made of cloud. She drew back; and from the phantom body her fingers had not touched, black blood was streaming.

The creature's smile was gone now. Its face was empty of surprise or anger: empty with a void so profound that Philip felt he could plunge into it and be lost.

Once again the air shivered with Linda's scream. This time she grasped for the creature's throat.

And beneath her hands the impalpable body began to fade. Its outlines blurred; the colors dimmed; its eyes were fixed, blind even to the face of its destroyer.

Then, like a storm cloud vanishing in the sunlight, it was gone. The echoes died; around them the air was clean.

For a long time the three who remained did not move. Then Linda turned, and Philip saw that the resemblance to Ygerna was now stamped indelibly upon her face. Neither his protection nor her resistance could help Linda any more.

He did not know if any difference now remained between her and the witch her sister; but love and pity filled his heart. "Linda," he said gently, "it's over now."

"Yes." She gave a faint, sad smile. "Yes, Philip, it's all over now."

"I gave her poppy-juice in the wine. She will sleep." The woman was black-haired and brown-skinned, with a young, kind face. She was Herne's sister.

Her eyes flickered to the stairway. From where they sat, they could look up to the open door of Linda's room. There, in a canopied bed with a black oaken chest at its foot, she lay in a drugged serenity. "How long has she been like this?"

"Three days, Helen." Herne's face was grave.

146

"In all that time she has not slept, for when she did she waked herself and us with nightmares."

"And you say this fever came over her after her struggle with the ghost? Small wonder in it! I have heard tell of warriors for whom such a contest ended in death or madness." Half to herself, she murmured: "Yet Linda survived. What is she, that such strength should be given her?"

Herne's eyes lifted to her face in quick recollection. He had asked that same question the night they lay in hiding and water came welling through the ground in answer to Linda's whispered words.

Philip looked about him. In this very kitchen— with its fireplace, its timbered walls, its windows set with panes of milky glass—Helen had looked up from her sewing on a day twelve years ago and seen her father watching her. Linda's father too. Philip came to a decision. "I will tell you what she is."

At once he had their full attention. Philip looked from one face to the other: so similar, so like Linda's as it lay, closed and still, against the pillow. "And forgive me that I have not told it sooner. But I was uncertain and troubled in mind. You were right, Herne, when you said she had not told you all the story. For Linda is half a witch. Her mother was Morgan; her father was your own. She is your sister."

He ended very quietly and looked down so he

need not see their faces. At last Helen spoke. "Poor child!" Her voice held only amazed compassion.

Herne looked up; his eyes were bright and hard. "Indeed, she deserves our pity. Yet what you have said, Philip, gives me a kind of horror of her."

"When all she did was to help us, you or me? The water when I was sick—risking her own life to defend us!" Philip stopped, astonished by the harshness of his indignation.

Herne bowed his head. "All this is true. But, Philip, what can we do now to rescue her? We are nearing the end of our journey, and there, you say, the witch is waiting. The time has come to decide what we must do."

Philip nodded. "For myself I have taken that decision. The witch in Linda has completely taken control—or, at least, she believes it has. She is in despair."

He paused, remembering her last drowsy words. Already the poppy-juice was working, but, her speech slurred with sleep, she had caught at his hand. "Philip. If you see my mother—"

At that word he turned and knelt beside her. "Morgan?" He whispered the name.

Her head moved fretfully against the pillow. "No, stupid, my *mother!*" Suddenly Philip remembered his gentle Aunt Margaret. "Yes."

"Tell her"—her voice was very soft now—"tell

her I love her. I don't think she always knew."

Philip lifted her hand and kissed it. "I'll tell her. And you'll tell her too."

But Linda only shook her head. "No . . ." she murmured, and, still clasping his hand, drifted into sleep.

Philip shook himself free of the memory, and spoke on. "There is only one power Ygerna fears, only one power equal to her own: the King himself. I will go to him for help. Only Kyril can save Linda now. We *must* reach him in time!"

11

Autumn lingered round the city where Kyril's palace stood, and a trace of autumn's gold still touched the fields—their grain mown into stubble—the orchards, and the vine-covered city wall. It was plain, reflected Philip, that no war had threatened here for many years, for the wall stood only as high as a man's breast, low enough for children to scale it in their games. It was built of rough, sun-warmed stone, its sand-color mellowed by the amber light.

No one challenged them at the gate. They rode across the square, a jostling mass of sound and color on this market-day, and along quiet, tree-shadowed streets cobbled with white stone. Leaves drifted downward, rustling on the wind; some already curled into brown shells, some still mottled with yellow, scarlet and orange. Harvest was over, but sometimes behind a rose-brick wall they glimpsed an orchard, with children scrambling for apples or windfall pears.

But always they sought the steeper streets, which led upward to the castle. From every point inside the walls it could be seen, with its windows of ruby glass and its square gray towers. It stood on a hill, surrounded by gardens and unfenced, untended meadows, where grass and wildflowers grew.

Presently Philip reined in his horse. "Linda, our ways part here."

"What?" She turned to him, dull wonder in her eyes. "Will you not come with me, Philip?"

"No." He shook his head, hardening himself against her sorrow at what she thought was his desertion.

"All alone, then," she said softly. "Well, good-by."

"Perhaps not good-by. Be fortunate and happy, Linda." It was a benediction: for the thought was in his mind that he might not see her again.

But she only shook her head. "I will be neither." With that she turned from him and rode on.

Herne hesitated. "Philip, I cannot leave her! She

cannot go alone!"

"Do what you must; but you go at your own peril."

Curtly Herne nodded. "That I know." Then he too was gone.

Closing his mind to sorrow, to all thought of the disaster that might be waiting, Philip spurred his horse into a gallop.

In a field outside the palace walls, Linda found the Tower of Orofyn. It stood alone, in ruins. She left her mare to wander at its will and walked slowly toward the door.

Herne saw her disappear into its darkness. Suddenly panic overcame him, and he began to run. "Linda!" he called. But at that instant a power—a power that had gripped him once before, in the November twilight of the forest—took possession of his body. For a few steps more he forced his legs to move; almost he had reached the ruins. Then will and strength forsook him, and he fell.

"I seek the King's help!" Philip swung down out of the stirrups. Guards surrounded him in the palace courtyard. "My errand is desperate!"

"What is your name, friend?" demanded their captain.

"Philip, a traveler out of the wilderness."

The captain nodded. "Come with me: we have

had word to let you pass."

So great was Philip's haste that he did not stay to marvel at Kyril's knowledge of him. The thought of what might even now be happening to Linda sent him running up the stairs in the captain's wake.

Linda, wandering in a dream, was not even aware of Herne's pursuit, did not know that he had fallen, conscious but paralyzed, outside the door. The tower rose around her, a shell of stone. Far above, the roof had tumbled inward: she could see a space of sky. Deep in its blue a bird was wheeling.

Before her stood a short flight of steps, which ended in a landing and another door. As she hesitated, looking upward, a form slowly gathered shape and substance before her eyes. Now Ygerna stood on the stone platform. She was as Linda remembered her, but her eyes were sunken deep, and her body had wasted so far that bones shadowed the translucent skin.

Somberly and in silence she gazed down at her half-sister. Then the apparition blended out of existence, and the landing stood empty. In the copse at the border of the field, a blackbird sang. Linda listened as though to a sound from another world. Then she began to climb the steps.

In a chamber whose windows were diamonds of

red and yellow glass, the King waited. Shadows ebbed and flowed around him, though torches burned in iron brackets along the walls. Philip, jostled among the guards, cast one swift glance at the man, robed in black velvet, who sat watching their approach. A carven chair served as his throne; only a shallow dais raised it above the level of the room. Then the crowd bore Philip forward. Suddenly he found himself before the steps.

He sank to his knees. The other men drew back, and Philip and Kyril were islanded in silence. Philip raised his head. "My lord—"

At the sight of that harsh, upswept face, amazement stopped his breath. *"My lord!"*

"I told you, Philip, that I had many names. Kyril Tessarion is the chief of them."

The man whom he had known as Leo leaned forward. "But for this moment let strangeness seem familiar. The task is not yet done."

"My lord, Linda is in danger! I beg you, help us!"

"Philip, you have journeyed all these weeks with one thought to sustain you: your determination to rescue Linda, even against her will. Would you have me save her now, or would you try your own courage?"

After a moment Philip stammered, "What can I possibly do?"

"A weapon lies ready. Look around you."

Dazed with astonishment and fear, Philip obeyed. Then he gave a cry of triumphant understanding. "The torches!" Springing up, he seized one from its bracket.

Kyril nodded. "Go, with my blessing. I will send my guard to clear the way. Captain! Philip, make haste!"

Once the room had been a lady's bower. Now the ruin of centuries had left it open to the sky. Above it rustled a network of branches, autumn-bare. The sunlight falling through them checkered the floor with gold and gray.

There Linda found Ygerna. In all the room there was nothing else but a table, a silver mortar, and a pestle made of bone.

They said no word of greeting. Instead Ygerna turned on her sister a look of ravenous questioning. In answer to that silence, Linda nodded. "I have it. I have brought it."

"Give it to me!" The words were ferocious in their longing. Ygerna snatched the box from Linda's hands and tore it open. At the sight of the indigo earth, she gave a long, low moan.

She emptied it into the mortar. Then she glanced sidelong at Linda. "I thank you, Sister."

"Your thanks are hateful to me. Fulfill our bargain."

Still Ygerna's voice was quiet. "Bargain? What

bargain did we make?"

"To return me, or at least Philip, to our own world!"

"*Your* world, Linda? You know well which is your world." Ygerna laughed. "And besides, your part of the compact is not yet fulfilled."

"I promised to bring you the Marrow!"

"You promised to bring me that which would restore my strength. You have found only one element. One is lacking."

Linda backed away. "What is it?" she whispered.

For a moment Ygerna considered her. "No, you are no true witch. Yet your power would grow greater, maybe, and challenge mine. Did you think, knowing that, that I would let you live?"

Her eyes were wide now, wide and laughing as a soulless creature's. "Linda," she said softly, "the second element is blood."

Without haste she came toward the girl. Her back was to the door. In her intentness, she did not hear the faint sounds on the landing outside. At that last instant, Linda's face gave her warning, and she whirled.

With a shout Philip was upon her. His torch dipped down; the flames caught Ygerna's dress; her long hair flared into a coronal of fire. The shriek she gave rang out over the fields, and all who heard it stood silent for a moment.

In that second the spell snapped, and Herne staggered to his feet. Philip came down the stairs, with Linda bundled in his arms. "Back! Away from the tower!" he cried.

The company of men, awed and murmuring, retreated from the walls. But now no voice could be heard, only the windy roaring of the flames. The stench of burning came to them, and through the shattered roof, smoke rose up to darken the clean sky.

When Linda looked into King Kyril's face, Philip saw her amazement and a brief, sudden joy. But at once she mastered it, or it died. "My lord, I come before you as a prisoner."

"What is this, Linda?" he demanded gently.

"She said to me 'Witches and witch-children— he spares none.' "

"Then she lied, as she lied about so many things. Come, rise, and sit beside me. You are weary."

But Linda remained on her knees before him. "I will not accept your mercy! I belong to no world now. Kill me, I beg you, for I have no wish to live." Her voice was ragged with strain; she had forced her last strength to this demand.

Kyril took her hands in a firm, gentle grip and drew her to her feet. "Your anguish speaks, and the self-hatred you have learned in these long weeks of doubt. Now, Linda, let me set your mind at rest. You are more human than you know."

Her fierceness had given way to a pitiful bewilderment. "But the spring—the demon—!"

Kyril nodded. "Powers you have, for your mother was indeed Morgan the Enchantress. But if you return to the world that has become your own, these powers will ebb, leaving you little more than ordinary mortals'. You can choose to let them go."

He took her face between his hands, and as once before, Philip saw her tension ease gradually into peace. "I confess that I doubted too. That was why, in your journey through the wilderness, I made certain you would find me. I needed to see Morgan's child, to discover how much of her mother's power she had inherited. You came, but you were closed against me. Yet one night something happened, and I found the answer I was seeking."

Down her cheek his finger traced the path of the single tear she had shed when he questioned her about her home. "I saw you cry. And, Linda, there was one thing Ygerna never told you. Try as she may, a true witch cannot weep."

12

They remained for many days at Kyril's court; and there they made friends and had adventures of which this story does not tell. The King created Herne a Ranger: one of the loyal huntsmen whose task it was to keep the wilderness free from evil things and to carry the royal justice into the wilder regions.

In all this time, Philip's anxiety for his cousin did not cease. He watched her closely and wished he could do something to drive the sadness from her face. At moments she would stand lost in thought, and if he dared to ask her why, she would evade the question with a gesture and an apologetic

smile. Still, her cheeks had grown less gaunt, and the pallor of her skin had changed to a healthy rose.

As the days passed, something would happen—a dance, a game, a song—to startle her out of her melancholy, and then it would be forgotten for a moment, a half-hour, and at last for hours together. Around them they found many young people of their own age, for Kyril, highly though he valued the grave wisdom of his counsellors, found pleasure in the company of the young. In front of one of the fireplaces that warmed the lesser hall (though, despite its name, it seemed imposing enough to Philip, with its timbered ceiling and its hangings of olive green) Linda would huddle against the chill, and in the narrow circle of warmth would practice dance-steps or a new song with her friends. Philip too enjoyed these gatherings, but most of all he enjoyed her self-forgetful pleasure. At other times they would ride out, ten or twelve in a company, to watch the falling leaves or shatter the ice-mirrors that night had crystallized on the surface of the pools. And then sometimes Philip heard Linda's laugh, as husky and strident as the laughter of an ordinary girl.

But a day came when the sky was a haze of snow-clouds, and all the beauty of autumn had gone by. As evening drew on, Kyril summoned the cousins to his private chamber. Philip found him seated by the window. The first stars of snow had just fallen on the ledge outside.

Philip bowed low. "My lord, Linda means no disrespect, but she begged me to tell you that she promised to dance with Thawn. She cannot come until her promise is fulfilled."

Kyril laughed. "Most proper! But I do not honor her too highly, for no doubt she enjoys paying such a debt. This is well, for I wished to speak to you alone. Sit down."

Philip took the stool beside him. Kyril's smile faded; his face was serious as he gazed down at his young guest. "But I think you know what I will say."

"You mean to send us home."

Kyril nodded. "Ygerna made a pact; it is for me now to fulfill it. But even if I offered it to you, Philip, would you choose to stay?"

Philip shook his head. "No, my lord. The strangest and most wonderful adventures of my life have happened here, but this is not my home."

"And what of Linda?"

For a long moment there was silence. At last Philip stirred and looked up at Kyril's face. Very quietly he replied, "You were right when you said that the thought of rescuing her sustained me. And at that time I didn't care whether she *wanted* to come back with me or not, because I was certain I knew what was best. Now . . ." He stopped and then with an effort continued. "I can't imagine being without her; I can't imagine what my uncle and aunt would say. But I know I cannot force her to return. She must make her own decision."

"I rejoice," said Kyril gently, "that you have grown in wisdom. For no human being can possess another, Philip: not even out of love."

The door opened, and Linda stood on the threshold. She made Kyril a deep curtsey; her cheeks were flushed from dancing. He smiled and held out his hand. "Welcome, Linda! Are you discharged of all your debts?"

"Yes, my lord!" She laughed and, running toward him, kissed the outstretched hand. "Why did you summon us?"

"The time has come to speak of your return."

Philip looked at her. "I've decided to go back, Linda."

Kyril said, "For Philip, the good sorrow of leave-taking is unmixed with doubt. He knows what he must do. But for you, Linda, the decision may not be so easy. Therefore, I ask you once again: which of the two worlds is your home?"

"Here I was born," said Linda softly, "and here I discovered what I truly am. I am grateful for that knowledge; perhaps a time will come when I can remember it without pain. But I don't *belong* here." She drew a deep, uncertain breath. "I've tried to persuade myself, but I can't. As a baby I might

164

have died but for the love Philip's family has shown me. I belong with them. If he goes, I will go with him."

Philip gazed at her in astonished relief. But Kyril answered, "You have chosen wisely. When I first learned of the two who had appeared in the wilderness, how little I hoped of either of you—a child of the witch Morgan and a boy, her adoptive cousin— a stranger not even of our stock! I too have grown in wisdom, for your courage has taught me much. No guest departs from us without a gift. Now I will give you mine. Philip, hold out your hands."

Philip extended them. Kyril's fingers closed around his wrists, and he felt a cool burning sensation, like a bracelet of white fire. When Kyril released his wrists, they bore his mark, as though his hands had burned them.

Then it was Linda's turn. When it was done, Philip said: "What is the meaning of this gift?"

"The lifetime that lies before you will reveal it; yet I will tell you a little. I have set my mark on you. Because of it, you will never be wholly severed from us, and in a time of great need it may be we shall meet again. Even if that never comes to pass, you will always see more deeply than others. Visions hidden from them will be revealed to you. And that is both a sorrow and a blessing."

He glanced toward the window where ghostly

flakes were drifting out of the darkness into the candlelight. "And now you must sleep, for it is late."

"Yes." Philip stifled a yawn. "I feel very tired suddenly. Perhaps it's all the decisions we've had to make."

"I should like to sleep now, too," said Linda, "if you will give us leave to go."

"You have my leave." Kyril laid his hands upon their heads. "And my blessing. Good night, my children."

13

Philip stirred. The bed beneath him felt hard as stone; his body was cramped from lying on it.

Then his eyes opened. The bed *was* stone, for he and Linda were lying on the rock shelf above the beach. Beside him, he saw her sleeping form, still covered by the space-blanket. In the half-light he could make out the rowboat drawn up on the shingle. He was wearing his jeans and sweater; above them the sky glowed rose and apricot with dawn.

"Linda!" The involuntary loudness of his cry echoed out across the water. From the farthest margin of the lake a loon's voice answered, then another and another, until four plangent, trembling voices took up their chorus among the silence of the hills.

She stirred. "Philip, I've had the strangest dream."

"*Not* a dream!" But everything disproved his words and turned them into illusions, into lies: the cabin that rose, solid and shuttered, on the opposite head of land; the gray mist coiling over the water; the smell of juniper, pungent in the dawn chill.

They pushed back the plastic blanket and stood up, looking dazedly around them. Linda gave a long, soft sigh. "We're home," she said.

Still Philip could not accept the evidence of eyes and ears and hands. He sat down and bowed his head. "He didn't even give us the chance to say good-by."

"Yes, he did, Philip." He heard strength and gentleness in Linda's voice, from which all sharpness had disappeared. "But we didn't understand."

"No. It's hard, though." Philip turned so that she would not see his face. A tear slid down onto the sleeve of his sweater. He wiped it away and stopped, arrested, staring. As he looked, his despair changed slowly to a still, triumphant joy.

For circling his wrists, faint and indelible as an ancient scar, he saw the mark of Kyril's hands.